ABSOLUTELY
HUGE

ABSOLUTELY HUGE

LUKE UPTON

y Lolfa

To Mum and Dad – thanks for everything

First impression: 2018

Cover image: Carl Pearce
Cover design: Sion Ilar

ISBN: 978-1-912631-01-8

Published and printed in Wales
on paper from well-maintained forests by
Y Lolfa Cyf., Talybont, Ceredigion SY24 5HE
website www.ylolfa.com
e-mail ylolfa@ylolfa.com
tel 01970 832 304
fax 832 782

Contents

Then

A WET AND cold Millennium Stadium, late November 2010.

Wales have huffed and puffed and even taken and held a first-half lead against New Zealand, but now trail 24-12 with 10 minutes to go. Some of the crowd have begun to trudge out of the ground, conscious of train queues, traffic jams and domestic promises. They have, after all, seen this all before.

The classic Welsh brave defeat.

In the rain.

A muted cheer emerges from the remaining crowd as the final two substitutions are made. Performances for their regions have seen both players talked up by the press this autumn, and injuries have seen them bumped into the match-day squad. Two callow youths about to make their debut, all-too-familiar fodder for friendly defeats.

"Please give a big Millennium Stadium welcome to two debutants: Emyr Glendower Jones-Parry replacing Mike J Davies, and Gethin Hughes taking the place of Nick Pratley."

You know what comes next. You are one of the 7,456,678 and counting who have watched the video on YouTube.

But let's hear those familiar lines again…

"Jones-Parry takes his place at 10 with Hughes
at 13."

> "I've been impressed by both of these this season,
> particularly Jones-Parry, but don't think the coach
> would have been looking to blood them against
> the All Blacks."

"No, I wouldn't have thought so – the toughest
of debuts. Very much a last roll of the dice from
Neil Malcolm here."

New Zealand kick off, and outside half Dave Blair drills the
ball deep into the corner of the Wales 22.

"Another good restart there, immediately
putting Evans under pressure."

Wales full back Mark Evans carries the ball forward a few
metres before getting hit by New Zealand winger Rich Te'fo
and centre Hemi Hinchcliffe and being thudded shoulder
first into the wet turf.

"Evans coming under a lot of pressure here,
just managing to get the ball away before
he could be pinged."

> "He did well there, but Wales immediately on
> the back foot again. They've been coughing
> up penalties all afternoon from kick-offs and
> are lucky to avoid another there."

"Rees. Digs it out and pops up Jones-Parry –
his first touch in international rugby. He takes
it up, gaining a few yards before scooping it in
to Garrett. Garrett goes round Michaels and into
some space just on the halfway."

> "Lovely little pass from the debutant there."

"Garrett comes back inside and offers it to

Hughes – a first touch for him too.
Hughes. Takes a step and rounds Leefo...
Suddenly a bit of space opens up on the left."

The crowd begins to stir, catching the whiff of a chance in the air.

"He's spotted a mismatch and Hughes goes
inside, then out, then back inside again."

Hughes has broken into the New Zealand half, turning two All Blacks inside out as he does. Used to a kicking game from the Welsh backs, the Kiwi defence isn't set up for a run from deep.

There's a clatter of chairs around the stadium as the fans stand for a better view.

"Hughes..."

Two All Blacks, Joni Nate and Noah Ayres, are coming at pace across the midfield to close down the space.

"...it's Hughes, still Hughes – he's got
Jones-Parry on his shoulder."

Those fans leaving the stadium stop on the stairs to watch.

He dummies to pass. Nate buys it, clattering an empty-handed Jones-Parry to the floor and winding him in the process.

One to beat.

"He shows the dummy and just has Ayres to
beat. He kicks it forward."

Space opens up in front of him.

The Millennium Stadium crowd begins to roar.

"It's a foot race, it's a foot race…"

Gethin Hughes and Noah Ayres hurtle down the left wing, arms flailing across each other, both hunting for an advantage with the ball five yards ahead of them.

Ayres, with his 74 caps and one World Cup, a qualified solicitor and future MP for Dunedin West.

Hughes – with only today's cap and three A-Levels – is however, at this moment, his equal.

"Hughes, hacks forward again, there's nothing between them."

The ball skips over the try line, the two men are intertwined but Ayres just has the edge as he dives upon the ball.

A low groan rolls out across the stadium.

"Ayres seems to have just abou–"

"Ohhh, wait…"

As Ayres dives forward, Hughes, just a fraction behind him, slips his right foot under the ball and in one fluid movement flicks it up out of the grasp of the New Zealand full back up and into the air.

"…Ayres is on the floor, but without the ball!"

The ball pops up into the hands of Hughes, who skips over the prone Ayres, nonchalantly glances back into the empty space behind him and with no one else within 20 metres, jogs over to the posts and dots it down.

"Try Hughes!"

"Wales try! Extraordinary."

As the cliché goes, the crowd goes wild.

The whole stadium is on its feet. The air is a jumble of triumphant fists, mobile phones and plastic pint glasses half full of Brains SA.

Even the New Zealand fans nod approvingly, some even smiling – they've seen plenty of great tries, but nothing quite like this.

"What a finish to a stunning run!"

"I've never seen a finish like that before. What a try for the 18-year-old Sailors centre. He started in his own half. And then to do that to a World Cup-winning full back. On your international debut. Well, wow – just wow."

"And now up steps Jones-Parry, wincing a little from his earlier tackle, to convert the easiest of kicks on his own debut.

It goes over. Wales 19 New Zealand 24 with 8 minutes to go. What a try we've just seen, and I can see the fans coming back up the stairs to retake their seats.

What a moment for young Gethin Hughes. He's proved himself in every game he's played since turning professional, and now he's done it for his country against the very best in the world."

"Remarkable – what have we got here?"

"Something very special. Something absolutely huge."

Now

THE CROWDS BEGAN to troop into Maes-y-Tawe RFC at about 5 o'clock, two and a half hours before his scheduled time of arrival.

Located on the edge of the village, the clubhouse is a long, thin, grey rectangular building with a sloping red roof, running parallel to the main pitch. The last landmark on the main road before the village drifts into farmland, it either welcomes you or waves you goodbye. One side is open, with large windows facing the car park and pitch, the other all brick. A limp Welsh flag flutters from a rusty pole. Over the door is a wooden sign, hand-painted but slightly peeling, giving you the name of the club, a *croeso* and also the logo of a former sponsor. R J Jones and Son Builder's Merchants went bankrupt in 2006, but they'd paid for the sign, so it was considered bad form to remove them from it.

Walk under the sign and through the double doors, and you are in the bar area. Still with the unspoken but persisting division of lounge versus bar, drinks are served at one end and television watched in the other. What you do if you sit in the middle is up to you.

Rebuilt in 1962 thanks to a donation from the local plastics factory (in apology for poisoning the local river), it has seen better days. Though the Committee intended this to be one such day.

It was the stalwarts of the Committee that arrived first. Ruddy cheeked and blazered, blow-dried and pearled, they were in their second home. Extra chairs were brought up from the cellar, the tables from the summer fete unfolded and dusted, and the raffle tickets checked and double checked.

Second came the media: a tight knit bunch, familiar from the television but always seeming shorter in real life. Shaking hands and exchanging easy laughs, while always keeping one eye on their smartphones. Lighting rigs went up and cable was taped down, as the best spots were secured for BBC and S4C. The TV crew that had come from Japan, already struggling without an interpreter, were shunted towards a spot in front of the disabled toilet.

The younger reporters discussed the best hashtag for the evening and took some photos of the recently polished trophy cabinet. A Glamorgan Shield from 1905, a county cup from 1946, a Swalec Bowl from 1985 and shirts and mementoes from long-departed touring teams circled the Welsh cap. Small but still fiercely red, it was the cap from his debut – the debut with THAT try.

Next up were the fans, the folk of the village, some setting foot in the clubhouse for the first time, others making a weekly or in some cases daily pilgrimage. The traditionalists arrived with a sniff, as they surveyed the busy scene and new faces before them. There were a few requests for the newcomers to move from long-established seats. Most grudgingly accepted.

The clubhouse had not been this busy since New Year's Eve 1999. A night when the good folk of Maes-y-Tawe feared the Millennium bug had struck when the power went out at the stroke of midnight. Five panicky minutes later and it was found that Stereophonicish (one of the top five Stereophonics tribute acts in south-west Wales) had rocked so hard they'd blown one of their amps and taken the whole fuse box with it.

What would loosely be described as the local 'faces' arrived next. The local MP, in the clubhouse for the first time since the last election campaign, guffawed through the door and headed straight for the journalists. Next came the Assembly Member and a gaggle of councillors, already animated. Some of the evening's attendees had met early in the Plough and Stars just across Parc Road for some early refreshment.

A ripple went round the room as Geert van Binder stepped in, ducking his head slightly to avoid the door frame. He nodded politely to a blazer on the raffle desk as he bought a pound's worth of pink tickets before heading to the rear of the room. It wasn't easy for a 6' 6" South African World Cup-winning lock and current Sailors Head Coach to act inconspicuously in a Swansea Valley rugby clubhouse. But he'd do his best.

Then came the waiting.

The locals ordered beers and chatted away. Snippets of the same conversation could be heard across the bar. Talk of 'waste' and 'luck', of Grand Slams and mountain rescues, penguins and Heledd Harte. The media eyed the beers but didn't dare order one – it wasn't like the old days, some of the veterans muttered ruefully. The bar didn't serve sparkling water. J2Os all round.

The MP strode over to van Binder and gave him a hearty handshake. His assistant took a photo of them together on her phone, a second farewell clasp ensued and the Honourable Member returned swiftly to the crowd of councillors.

Van Binder stared into the trophy cabinet, barely recognizing any of the names on the dusty pennants and faded shirts. He spotted mementoes from France, Italy, Romania, even Uruguay. So many visiting teams had come to this small Welsh town from all the over the world. He thought back to his own first club, similar to here in many ways. Though no international visitors had come to South Africa in the 1980s. His eyes came to rest on the cap in the middle: it seemed small, almost comically so. It wouldn't have fitted on his head, would it?

A round of flashes from cameras and smartphones snapped van Binder out of his daze. He turned to look out into small car park. A silver Range Rover had parked by the door, and three men stepped down from it. The crowd in the bar instinctively took a step forward as they saw he was among them.

A hush descended as the trio headed towards the door.

First in was Gary Johns, his agent. A semi-professional snooker player turned radio DJ, turned sports agent, turned who-knows-what now. He'd given a lot of bad advice and the Establishment had little time for him any more.

Nonetheless, few men stepped into Maes-y-Tawe RFC in a white suit, pink shirt and yellow tie. Gary Johns was such a man.

Following Gary was Alun 'Polaris' Protheroe, the Chairman of Maes-y-Tawe, a forty-year veteran of the club, and unlikely 1970s nuclear submariner. Polaris was now in his late 60s, his dark blazer with the club crest – the river, the hill behind the village and the long-departed plastics factory jostling for space on the stitching – fitting snugly around his well-fed belly.

Polaris moved towards the microphone, which had been

set up in front of a large blank projector screen. Usually used for Welsh internationals, Premier League football and the *X-Factor* final, tonight's entertainment would be a combination of all three.

He cleared his throat and the boisterous room of around 300 club members, locals, media and the generally nosy fell quiet.

"Welcome everybody – many thanks for coming out tonight. Great to see so many of you are here. Where were you for the game against Llyn Hendre on Saturday?"

A few coughs and murmurs rolled across the crowd.

"Well, we've had some exciting moments at this club and we are very excited about today. We've always been proud to develop our own, and when one returns it is always an honour. Especially one with such talent. I saw him make his debut here when he was just 16. And we all remember his international debut, and the years that followed for the Sailors, Wales and the Lions..."

"Moooooooooooooooooo," reverberated suddenly from the back.

Laughs echoed around the room.

One of a group of local lads towards the rear of the bar, not long in from a shift at the local call centre, was particularly proud of his contribution to the evening. A high five was offered across the table and the bovine impressionist happily obliged.

"...Yes, and of course there have been ups and downs, as there are in any career. But the important thing is..."

"Mooooooooooooo," again from the back.

"Please gentlemen, let's show some respect," stuttered a reddening Polaris.

The boys, emboldened by the reaction, were about

to repeat the noise again, when van Binder, standing diagonally across from the table, coughed and caught the eye of the table leader. He fixed him with a glare, the one that had once intimidated his Kiwi opposite number in a World Cup final. The table fell silent.

"Thank you. Well, I don't think our new signing needs too much of an introduction. But just in case... hit it, Catrin."

Suddenly the room went dark.

The large screen flickered on.

The video began to roll.

Images began to flicker on the screen. Him as a youngster at the club: all spiky blond hair, and still a little chubby.

Then there he is playing for Wales on his debut: shirt too big, but scooping up the ball with his foot after that amazing bit of skill.

More tries followed – a dazzling array of movement and skill in a variety of jerseys from rainy pitches in Ireland to the highveld in South Africa. A drop goal versus Australia sailing highly and narrowly over the posts. The roar as he lifts the Six Nations trophy. Being mobbed by teammates after that try-saving tackle against England.

Then came some stills from modelling shots, promotional images, a few generous paparazzi pictures and even one from *Farmer's Gold*, of him dressed in tweeds with a piglet under each arm.

A very muted "Mooooooooooo" echoed from the darkness.

The action shots slowed, the modelling shots continued, plus some with the nation's sweetheart, Heledd Harte.

The video stopped abruptly on an image of him being winched into an RAF helicopter on the side of Mount Snowdon, holding an oversized spoon.

17

And the lights blinked back on.

"Well thank you, Catrin, for that very impressive clip show. Your Media Studies teacher will be very impressed," said Polaris, taking to his feet.

"Okay, well, I think that's got you in the mood. And I am delighted to welcome, and please be upstanding for, the pride of Maes-y-Tawe returning to the club – Mr Gethin Hughes!"

He stepped through the door, a little gingerly, giving a few little smiles as he passed through the crowd, making his way to the front. Dressed in a blue shirt and chinos – 'smart casual' – a gift from a Cardiff clothes shop during his Wales days.

Hughes reached the front, shook Polaris' hand and turned to the room. The blond hair a bit shorter than in his prime and slightly broader across the chest, he had, however, managed to maintain most of his shape from his playing peak. The cameras flashed and some of the journalists began shouting questions. But the requests for quotes were soon drowned out by shouts of "Huge, Huge, Huge" from the Maes-y-Tawe supporters.

It was like old times. Almost.

Gethin gave a big smile, leant into the microphone and uttered his first public comment in over 18 months.

"Hiya."

Ten years after making his debut for the club, and just three years after last playing for his country, former Wales and British and Irish Lions star Gethin 'Huge' Hughes was back playing for Maes-y-Tawe, in WRU Division 5 South Central (C) of the Welsh pyramid.

How the hell did this happen?

CHAPTER ONE

Genesis

"It's home, like. Sure it's not a big city like New York or Swansea.
And it hasn't got a cinema, or a Nandos, which is a shame.
But it's where I'm from. It's where I first played rugby.
Where I learnt the basics. Where my mum and dad are.
And I guess, where I'm back again now."

"Scoring those tries, getting all the pats on the back and
seeing what I could do when I was in the backs made it all click.
From that day I was hooked. It was rugby all the way."

THE ONLY OTHER famous person from Maes-y-Tawe described the little Swansea Valley town as 'a small blurry dump, surrounded by brown blurry hills and trees, with grey blurry people.'

In his 1987 autobiography, *Burning down the Zeitgeist Tower*, Edmund de Turin (born Edward Rees on Chapel Street in 1936), had paid little heed to the town where he was born and lived until the age of nine, when his family emigrated to New York. For one of the foremost voices in post-war US art criticism, Maes-y-Tawe had played only a small part in his life. But for Gethin 'Huge' Hughes, his home village was, and continues to be, a major influence in his story.

A town of around 8,600, it's nestled on both banks of the River Tawe around 30 minutes north of Swansea. Like most towns in the South Wales Valleys, it was a small grouping of farms until the Industrial Revolution transformed the area, bringing first coal mining, then copper smelting. The population swelled with families coming from across Wales, and further afield, to the collieries and works. When coal and copper began to wane, plastics filled the gap, with a large factory employing 550 workers at its peak, before closing in 1998.

Now most of the Maes-y-Tawe locals work in the small enterprise zone, a call centre, the town's shops or commute to Swansea or even Cardiff. 9.8% of the town's adults don't work at all.

But compared to some other nearby towns, it's not doing too badly at all. There's still a good community feel. The hills looming over the town are green and lush, something that still surprises the old timers when they remember them rusty and bare in the last days of heavy industry. The town's religious inhabitants have consolidated themselves into respectable congregations at the two remaining chapels. Shops work harder at their window displays and the pubs are doing decent food. One even does Thai. It's doing okay. And then there's the rugby.

Maes-y-Tawe RFC has been a fixture in the town's life since it was founded by workers at the copper plant in 1904. In its 110+ years of fielding teams, it has weathered industrial upheaval, world wars, mass unemployment and the growth of the twin evils of 5-a-side football and computer games with solid deference.

Always languishing towards the bottom of the Welsh rugby pyramid but never seeming to mind that much, it's a club with a focus on young players and post-game hospitality as much as the 80 minutes on a Saturday afternoon. It has two senior teams, an A and B, plus age-group teams down to U12s. Plus a women's team that plays when it can find opponents. They all play at Parc Park, an historically unimaginative name, but one that keeps both the town's Welsh speakers and the lazy happy.

One of the mainstays of the 1920s Maes-y-Tawe team was George P Hughes, better known as 'Stumpy'. A solid second row, he played over 200 games for the club and achieved some minor South Wales celebrity through an incident that occurred in a cup game against Caermorris in 1925. Stumpy acquired his nickname on account of playing all his games for Maes-y-Tawe with a wooden leg, having lost his original one at the Battle of Jutland in 1916. The fixture, a local derby, was always a very physical encounter. Towards the end of the match, with the scores tied, Stumpy was hit by such a ferocious tackle that his wooden leg came out of its setting and fell to the floor. A brawl ensued and local reports state that the felled Stumpy hopped up on his one remaining leg and struck his tackler several times across the head with his prosthetic. The local rugby administrators were up in arms about it, but the press loved the story.

Newspapers across the world wrote about this plucky injured veteran, and there was even a popular Welsh music hall song composed about the incident – 'Peg Leg! *Chwarae Teg!*' But as a war hero, Stumpy avoided punishment, continuing to play for several more seasons, and was reportedly rarely tackled from then on, for fear of the consequences.

And it's into this town that Stumpy's great-grandson Gethin Andrew Hughes was born at 8.01 a.m. on Tuesday 9th June 1992. The second of four children, he appeared early and quickly at just eight months, surprising his mother at the school where she taught, Derwen Primary. Mrs Hughes gave birth in her classroom early one morning as she was preparing the day's classes, leading to the school being closed that day.

Even at one day old, Gethin Hughes was already popular among the town's youngsters.

Gethin's mum, Helen, had met Gethin's dad, Mike, on a night out in Cardiff in the early 1980s. Married a few years later, Mike's work as a council surveyor brought him back to his hometown of Maes-y-Tawe, and they began a family. First came Rhys (now a teacher in Cardiff), then Gethin, followed by Teleri (a hairdresser in Swansea) and finally Louise (an accountant in Dubai).

A lively and sporty family, they all grew up on the pitches of Maes-y-Tawe RFC, where Mike was a regular in the B team for much of the children's early years. A solid number eight, he was a long-serving member of the squad and was and is a familiar figure around the town. And much of Gethin's early life was focused around the rugby club:

"I guess my earliest memories are of being at Parc Park. Going there was always a treat, not that I was that interested in rugby at first. More because Mum would always buy us donuts to keep us entertained when Dad was playing. There'd normally be five in a bag, and four of us, so we'd create little competitions to win the fifth. I remembering tripping up Tel while racing one day, and her hitting me so hard with her Barbie doll that I got a black eye. No one got the extra donut that day. Guess we were all pretty competitive from the start!"

Gethin started at King Edward's Road Primary in 1996. A popular and highly energetic pupil, he was at times hard to control in class, always impatient to get out into the yard in the breaks and lunch to run around.

In those first years at school the young Gethin wasn't that interested in rugby.

His first love was wrestling, particularly the American version packed full of razzmatazz and big stunts. So fond of it was the young Gethin that at eight years of age, he started calling himself Captain Gethin and wearing a cape made of his nanna's old curtains paired with a back-to-front baseball cap, and doing wrestling moves on friends and family. It was the Captain persona that would lead to his first but certainly not last major injury, as school friend Michael James tells us:

"It was a wet play… sorry, that's when it's raining so badly that you can't go out into the yard so have to play in the hall. We were all running round, swapping Premier League stickers, the usual, when suddenly there was Gethin at the very top of the pile of gym equipment in the corner. His best mate, Gaz, was lying on a mat underneath him shouting 'C'mon, c'mon!' He was always a bit of nutter was Gaz, and he loved this kinda stuff. Suddenly Gethin dived off the pile, aiming for Gaz. Like one of those wrestlers on Sky, y'know? I don't know quite what happened, but he missed Gaz. Missed the mat and landed on the wooden floor. There was a terrible crack and he'd broken his arm. He sorta passed out, I think. Some of the girls started crying, and the boys started shouting 'Miss! Miss! Gethin's dead, Gethin's dead!' The teachers came running inside and he went off to hospital. He wasn't dead, but his arm was a right state. Funnily enough I saw Gaz the other day – he's a health and safety officer down the steel works now. Must have had some effect on him too."

The broken arm put paid to Gethin's dream of professional wrestling. But when school started back up the following year, rugby made its first appearance. Year Five was when the King Edward's Road Primary children could first play competitive rugby, and Gethin Hughes made his rugby debut versus Crosston Primary School. Little did rugby know on that rainy Tuesday in September 1997 that a legend who would change the world of rugby forever was making his debut.

The match was abandoned after eight minutes because of a hailstorm, with the score at 0–0. But nonetheless, Gethin was on the way.

That season, a chunkier-than-we-are-familiar-with Gethin played as hooker. It took him a while to get to grips with that position but he was already amongst the tries, picking up eight in that first year, which made him the second top try scorer in the team. But he wasn't always a natural at the getting points for his team as his first coach, and deputy head, Ieuan Moretti lets on:

"I can't quite remember who we were playing, but we were hammering them, 20, 30 points up. We could already see that Gethin was an excellent player. He caught the ball on an interception and ran the length of the pitch. He had time to turn and grin towards us as he did. I'll always remember that. But unfortunately, he just kept on running. He went over the try line then carried on running straight on and dived over the dead-ball line, taking the ball out of play as he grounded it. He got up and started celebrating it and everything. All the boys were cracking up. To be honest, me and the ref were laughing too. It was pretty funny. He got called Forrest after Forrest Gump for a while after that."

When he was 11, Gethin made the move a mile up the road to Maes-y-Tawe Comprehensive. His brother Rhys was already there, and being the only secondary school in the town, nearly all his class moved with him. He started playing rugby immediately, making the Year Seven first XV, and also now playing age-grade games for Maes-y-Tawe RFC. By this stage Gethin had moved from the front row to the back row as an energetic number eight, and although certainly one of the best players in both teams, few would have marked him out in his early teens as a superstar in the making.

Rugby was still not the dominant interest in Gethin Hughes' life. In his early teens, it ran a close third behind skateboarding and rollerblading. Whilst Maes-y-Tawe lacked a halfpipe, Gethin and his mates would use bits of abandoned heavy industry that were scattered around the town to skate off. His major influences were reflected in his clothing, a unique mix of baggy shorts, skateboard shoes and rugby top, and the walls of his bedroom were covered with pictures of Tony Hawk rather than Rob Howley.

No one would say that Gethin was a model pupil.

Although largely popular with pupils and teachers, he was easily distracted, lacking focus in the classes which bored him. He liked to play the clown and, with a natural gift for mimicry, his impressions of teachers got him an equal mix of laughs and detentions. Aside from rugby and PE, there was only one class that held his attention – English Literature. One of his teachers, Mrs Samantha Brown, remembers one particular class where this passion came to the surface:

"Gethin's probably the most famous person to come out of the town. So when I'm on holiday or at a conference or something and say where I'm from, I sometimes get asked about him. I say I taught him and they ask about rugby. But I don't pay attention to that. What I remember is one day when we were doing the Dylan Thomas poem, 'Fern Hill'. I asked Gethin to read it aloud, to begin the class. He did the first few lines fine, and then seemed to begin slowing and choking up a little bit. I asked if he was OK, he said he was and carried on, but soon he was slowing again. I looked at him and he was crying. Little tears were coming down his face. As he got to 'And as I was green and carefree, famous among the barns…', he said, 'Sorry, Miss,' burst into tears and ran out of the door.

Everyone was a bit stunned, but he came back five minutes later and sat back down. Someone else was reading by then, and he seemed OK. I asked him to stay behind at the end of class. Kids often bring their problems from home into class and I wanted to see if he was OK. He looked a bit sheepish, then said it was the poem and that it was too sad. He burst into tears again. The PE teachers have some very different anecdotes about him, but mine is him crying at 'Fern Hill'."

I asked Gethin about this:

"No, don't remember that. Didn't happen. Not going to cry at a poem, am I? And anyway I prefer R S Thomas."

Through his early years in Comprehensive, Gethin was a good but not great schools player. He had made the number eight position his own between the ages of 11 and 15, being part of a moderately successful team and balancing the skateboarding and poetry with his rugby. Few would have marked out the increasingly lanky back-row forward as a future British and Irish Lions number thirteen.

Perhaps one of the pivotal moments in his career came

when the starting outside centre was suspended from school for setting up a false account on an online dating site with the headmaster's photo and contact details. He protested that the headmaster had asked for his help to do it. But suspension from school also meant exclusion from all sporting teams, so he was out. A cup semi-final against Llanowen Boys School was looming, and with a few other injuries and absences, a selection crisis hit the back line. As a talented ball handler, it was Gethin who was selected to fill the spot vacated by the digital prankster.

Llanowen had won the Swansea Valleys Schools Association Cup the previous two years. And are remembered by those I spoke to at Maes-y-Tawe as one of those teams that looked about three years older than everyone else. Geraint Jeffs, a teammate of Gethin's, remembers this fixture well:

> "They used to batter us. Every time. I'm not exaggerating. One year, their bus pulled up and the captain was driving it. He must have been fourteen at the time. Even the teachers were scared of him. They all seemed to have beards. Most of them smoked. Marlboro Reds. Unfiltered. They normally lit up when their kicker was taking a penalty or conversion. I remember one of them bringing his kid to a game as he couldn't get a babysitter. He just put the cot down amongst the tackle bags and got on with the game. We were like little boys against them until Gethin joined the team. I'm in the police now, and I reckon I must have arrested at least half of that Llanowen side. The other half are on the force with me."

Early onset facial hair and 20-a-day habits didn't help Llanowen that day. Inspired by a Gethin hat trick from outside centre, Maes-y-Tawe won 32–10 and he would never play in the pack again. Gethin takes us through the importance of that day:

> "I guess until that day, I enjoyed rugby the same way I liked skateboarding, watching DVDs or MSN Messenger. It was something to do with my mates. But that day, scoring those tries, getting all the pats on the back and seeing what I could do when I was in the backs made it all click. From that day I was hooked. It was rugby all the way."

Maes-y-Tawe won the final, their first trophy in 18 years, with Gethin landing two tries. At that final, played at Neath's Gnoll ground, there were a number of scouts from the Welsh clubs and national selectors and another Man of the Match performance had Gethin's name firmly noted in each of their notebooks.

It was not until the following season, when Gethin was established as an outside centre, that the first interest from a professional team appeared. Ten games into the season, he'd scored 24 tries and had even landed a few extravagant drop goals for his school. But more tellingly, he'd been bumped up the age groups at Maes-y-Tawe RFC and, at 16, was the newest and youngest member of the second XV.

This was tough, hard rugby, playing against men who were two, sometimes three times his age and for whom the 80 minutes on a Saturday were a way of getting all the stress and frustration of the working week out of their system. But the tries kept on coming for the second XV – three in one game, five in another – and soon he was knocking on the door of the first XV.

His club coach was Dai Newell, who became a big early influence on Gethin. A policeman and former 800 m runner for Wales, he put a major emphasis on fitness, focus and in his own words 'not fuckin' about' in training or in games. He was reluctant initially to put Gethin in the first team:

> "I've known Gethin all my life, having played with his dad. And at 16 he was a real talent. Quick and strong in the tackle, with a great pass, and an eye for the try line. I knew he was good. But I didn't want to put him into the first team straight away. He still had a lot to learn and sometimes he could be a bit funny... well, one day we were getting ready for training and as we were running out, the heavens opened. We started warming up and I noticed Gethin wasn't there. I sent one of the lads into the sheds to see where he was but he came back without him. I asked what was up and he said Gethin had told him he'd just put a new gel on his hair and he wasn't sure if it was waterproof so wanted to wait for the rain to stop. Apparently he'd imported it from Japan and didn't want to waste it. It wasn't even a game, it was bloody training! I'd never heard the likes of it! I sent him home, and he didn't play that Saturday. But... no, soon enough he was playing for the first team. He was so good, I just couldn't not pick him."

Gethin's first-team debut took place on December 8th, 2008 against Ystradcarew. Lining up alongside his geography teacher, Rhys Cooper, at centre, it generated a bit of a buzz in the village. At 16 years and 182 days, Gethin was the youngest player to play for the club's first team since Evan 'Bach' Reeves had done so at the uncorroborated age of 13 years and no days in 1918. The local paper. the *Maes-y-Tawe Gazette*, was there to record the event:

RUGBY NEWS

10th December 2008

Maes-y-Tawe 27-Ystradcarew 9

A debut brace of tries for youngster Gethin Hughes saw the Maes record a fine victory over near-neighbours Ystradcarew, writes Bill Williams. In front of a season-best attendance just short of 90, the Maes delivered one of their strongest showings in recent memory. After a cagey opening period, with both sides trading penalties, debutant Gethin Hughes broke through some weak tackling in the centre of the park, handed off one defender then rounded the full back before going over in the corner. Bryn Michaels rumbled over from a scrum to make it 17-3 at half-time.

Two penalties in close succession from the visitors threatened to make a game of it before Hughes grabbed his second, intercepting a loose pass from the Ystrad scrum half before running 40 yards to make the game safe. Rich Adams added the extras and a further late penalty. Man of the Match was Gethin Hughes – although he is not old enough to drink the bottle of sparkling wine, so gave it to his mother, Derwen Primary Headmistress Mrs Helen Hughes. Next up at Parc Park is Rhos North on 22nd December with the Christmas Quiz to follow. Teams of five, please see Viv for details of how to enter.

Parc Park. Attendance 86,
referee Lewis Morgan (Hendy).

Maes – Tries: Hughes x2, Michaels; Cons: Adams x2; Pen: Adams.

Ystradcarew – Pens: Hulme x3.

Another impressive debut saw Gethin become a first team regular, the youngest in the entire league. The games and the tries continued to flow for school and for club, and he was called up for the Swansea Schools U18s, again as one of the youngest players. Confident performances for the representative team led naturally to the next call, one from a professional team.

Since the difficult birth of professional rugby in Wales, the league and system had undergone a number of changes, but by the time Gethin got the call, it had settled down, grouped around five professional super-clubs competing in the Celtic League and European competition, and whose players make up the bulk of the Welsh national squad.

In 2009 the five were the Capitol Kings, based in Cardiff;

Gethin's local region, the Sailors, from Swansea; the Gwent based Borderers; the West Wales outfit, Y Gorau (Welsh for 'the best'); and the newest addition, Criccieth RFC in North Wales. It was Criccieth who moved first for Gethin, sending scouts to his games and making sure they met his parents in the clubhouse.

Criccieth RFC are an unlikely addition to the top table of Welsh rugby, based as they are in a small seaside town near Mount Snowdon. Until a few years ago, they played at a level below even Maes-y-Tawe. But this all changed when one of their former youth players, Iolo Daniels, sold his stake in a microchip he'd helped develop and which is found in every mobile phone in China, for £1.6 billion. A tech investor since he was 14 years old, he is reported to have been the seventh person to ever use a hashtag.

On becoming a billionaire, Iolo relocated from Hong Kong to the Bahamas, but not without investing in his childhood club. His money built a new stadium with a capacity of 28,000 in a village with a population of 1,800. This new stadium became not only the largest club ground in the country, but ever the renaissance man, Iolo ensured it included an art-house cinema, an organic supermarket and the largest bikram yoga studio outside New York. He then filled the team with professionals who propelled the club quickly and easily up through the league pyramid.

When the 'super clubs' were being decided, the WRU originally planned for four. But Iolo wanted Criccieth RFC to be a fifth. Initially rebuffed by the Welsh rugby hierarchy, exactly what happened next has never been confirmed. But the accepted version of events seems to be that Iolo asked them to name a price. They named an astronomical figure. Iolo wrote a cheque.

And as a result, this small village from the north has

a team competing alongside the famous names and large cities and towns of the south. This famous cheque also secured Iolo a 12-foot bronze statue of himself outside the National Stadium: rugby ball in one hand, microchip in the other and usually on match days a traffic cone on its head.

A formal offer was made, inviting Gethin to Criccieth for a few days to train with the Academy, get a feel for the club and area and see how he'd fit in with them. And so began one of the first classic Huge stories. We'll let Gethin share what happened next:

"Well, I had the offer from Criccieth to go up for a couple of days to scope it all out. Mum and Dad were both working, Rhys was away at university and Tel and Lou both had school so they agreed for me to go up on my own. I got up there on the Sunday and was meant to start doing some training on the Monday. So I was having a wander around on the Sunday afternoon. There's not much to do like, so thought I'd go to the castle. I always quite liked this kinda stuff, so was looking at the model castles and the film about Gerald of Wales. I was wandering around and suddenly the lights went off as I entered this little room and the door slammed behind me. It was pitch black in there. I was trying the door but it wouldn't open. I began shouting for someone to come and help me, but they didn't. The battery on the Nokia had died. I couldn't believe it: I was trapped in the dungeon!

I had to stay in there all night in the dark, with no food or drink or anything. It was pretty horrible. I was cold. And starving. And heard some weird noises… no, not ghosts… no… but they were odd. I don't think I slept at all and but at some point the following morning, I heard the keys to the door rattling, and suddenly the lights went on as the staff arrived.

Turns out I hadn't been locked in a dungeon, I'd been

trapped in the gift shop. As I looked around, I saw I could have had a feast of Welsh cakes, waffles and fudge! But I had no time for that. I wasn't in a great state and had to go straight to training with Criccieth. It didn't really go very well.... so yeah, that was about that with them, really."

The training session, to which Gethin arrived an hour late, did not go well. Tired, hungry and occasionally whispering about having seen a 'White Lady' whilst in the gift shop, he performed poorly in the session. The Criccieth RFC senior coaching team – headed by William Taylor-Shaw, OBE, the former England coach who had recently been lured from Twickenham to Gwynedd for a reported £2.5m-a-year pay packet – didn't like what they saw. And they had a boatload of Fijians arriving that afternoon. They didn't need a lethargic, pale-looking lad from the south blabbering about ghosts. Gethin was sent home after lunch, never to return.

At a £1000-a-ticket charity fundraiser in 2014 for the Iolo Daniels Foundation, a charity focused on maintaining the health of the nation's Cardigan Welsh Corgis, the subject of Gethin came up. In front of the great and the good of Welsh society, the *Western Mail* reported that the billionaire was asked during a Q and A about the failure of Criccieth, at that time European Cup holders, to sign up the young Gethin Hughes, and Iolo replied in typical fashion:

"I've added many of the most important Welsh artifacts to my museum in Criccieth. The bottle that held the 18th straight whisky that killed Dylan Thomas, Shakin' Stevens' denim jacket from the 'This Ole House' video, Reverend James' favourite tankard, the other twin from *Twin Town*. I've got it all in my collection. But there's one item that's slipped through my fingers: Huge. We didn't get him then, and we have yet to see him run out in the classic pink, green and orange of Criccieth… but he's still young, and I'm still fabulously rich. Let's see, shall we?"

This wouldn't be the last time Iolo and Gethin's paths would cross.

Back in South Wales, Gethin returned to school and club rugby but word had spread to his home region, the Sailors, that a prospect just half an hour's drive north of their home stadium was worth investigating. The game that the Sailors' Academy Director Matt Draper came to see, though, wouldn't be the easiest in which to gauge Gethin's skills:

"I'd heard plenty about Gethin – word spreads pretty quickly on the rugby grapevine. I thought we'd lost him to Iolo's little project up in Criccieth, but then he locked himself in a haunted house or something and ended up back home. So I drove up one Wednesday night for a cup game that Gethin was starting. But when I got up to Maes-y-Tawe, it was absolutely chucking it down, proper *bwrw hen wragedd a ffyn*, as my mam would have said. Anyway, I'm standing under the canopy of the club house, Gethin and the lads are all out on the pitch and the ref is talking to both captains ahead of the kick-off. Suddenly he runs off, leaves the pitch and gets in his car, parked on the halfway line. I think he's leaving. But then he beeps his horn and the game kicks off. At the first breakdown, he flashes his right indicator to indicate home ball. Turns out he's bloody refereeing from his car! I think he must have done it before – he's got his own system. Turning on his brake lights means forward pass, full beams equals a knock on and when a try was scored he wound down the window and turned up the radio for 10 seconds. The players seemed kind of used to it. I've never seen anything like it. At the end of the game, he just hit the horn three times and drove off! I was a bit distracted by this, but Gethin made a big enough impression and caused the referee to wind down his window three times, so I think he scored a hat trick. We knew we wanted him."

The invite came shortly afterwards to train with the Sailors, and this time Gethin's father drove him every day, he avoided the charms of any of the area's castles, and after five days' training with the Academy, was offered a contract with the region.

The Sailors at this time had a reputation for having a core of talented but hard-partying players. Under the stewardship of Owen Rhys, they thrived on this reputation, and were expected to overtake Y Gorau as the dominant club force in Wales. It was to this squad that a 17-year-old Gethin Hughes was added.

The professional journey had begun. Huge was a Sailor.

CHAPTER TWO

Setting Sail

"From the moment I saw him, I knew we had something special.
Trouble is, he knew it too."

"With a few minutes to go, we had another scrum and he kept
shouting 'swap, swap'. So I just thought: well, we are losing –
if that's what the kid wants, let him do it."

THE SAILORS THAT Gethin joined was the best supported of
the five Welsh regions and a regular supplier of players to
the national team. But since their founding in 2002, they
had become most famous for two things: losing big games
and disciplinary problems off the field.

They had never won a trophy.

The previous season had seen them lose in the infamous
'helicopter final' of the Celtic League to Criccieth RFC.
Iolo Daniels, running late, landed his helicopter (an exact
reproduction of one Tom Jones used in Las Vegas in the
1970s) on the pitch shortly before a first-half Sailors penalty
that would have put them 10-3 up. The game was delayed
by 15 minutes whilst Iolo chatted to the players and his
luggage, which included a pet zebra and a Leonardo da Vinci
sketch, was unloaded. Once successfully disembarked, the
pitch had to be repaired and an eminently kickable penalty

just outside the Criccieth 22 was missed. A furious WRU fined Iolo £125 (suspended) for his disruptive arrival. The Sailors didn't score any more points and a 23-7 victory for Criccieth was also ensured by the previous week's signing of five All Blacks, all of whom returned straight home after getting their medals.

The Sailors had also suffered a reverse in the Semi Final of the European Plate to Connaught after being 18-3 up at half-time. Rival fans, social media and even some sections of the press revelled in their nickname of Failors.

Then there were the boozy nights out.

Pubs and clubs from across the region were all too familiar with the squad piling in en masse, irrespective of that day's result. The mantra of 'win or lose – get on the booze' which professionalism was meant to have eradicated was still key to the Sailors' identity.

One particular incident in Tenby in 2009 has gone down in Welsh rugby legend. What precisely happened has never been fully established, with the players keeping to a strict code of silence, but between posts on social media, camera phone photos, rumours in the town and a police report, we can plot the following series of events.

After a 22-12 defeat to Y Gorau in Llanelli, the then Sailors captain Owen Rhys organized a night out in this popular and picturesque tourist town on the Pembrokeshire coast. Arriving straight from game, the evening would be what the players called a 'Three Course Meal' – a steak dinner followed by pub crawl, with a curry to finish.

At some point in the seventh pub of the 'main meal' – the Three Mariners Inn – and before the curry 'dessert', several of the Sailors squad got into conversation with the crew of a trawler, the *Catrin-Mae*, which worked out of Tenby harbour. Shortly after 11 o'clock, while the rest of the squad headed on to the Bay of Bengal curry house, five of the squad, including captain Owen Rhys, decided to head elsewhere.

Around two hours later Dyfed Powys Police receive a call from a panicky monk on Caldey, a small island about half a mile across the water from Tenby and the home of a Cistercian Monastery. Brother Ignatius was reporting 'a group of five large men in the Abbot's Kitchen (the island's fudgery), who appeared to have turned all the machines on, were making lots of noise and were scaring some of the elderly monks.'

The site of a monastery since 1906, this was the first time that a 999 call had ever been made from Caldey Island. The recording of the call reported that the monks had initially tried an exorcism, but that these weren't devils as initially feared – in fact these unwelcome visitors were all too human.

The police boat was launched, with reinforcements sought out from nearby villages in anticipation of a potentially major incident. One junior PC, suspecting that Al Qaeda had come to Pembrokeshire, insisted on bringing a cricket bat as a weapon. But on arrival at the fudgery, the officers, according to the police report, found not terrorists but instead: "Five adult males, sleeping on the floor in a state of clear post-intoxication. It appears there had been unsuccessful attempts to use the machines, and several empty fudge and chocolate packets were scattered around the males."

No charges were ever brought.

And there is no evidence that these five intruders were members of the Sailors squad.

Incidentally, two weeks after those unknown individuals disturbed the peace of the holy island, the monks of Caldey were guests of honour at the Black Rock Stadium for the Sailors' fixture against Ulster. In front of a somewhat confused crowd, 14 monks in their distinctive black and white cloaks and habits did a pre-match lap of honour around the pitch and Abbot Daniel blessed the ball before announcing on a microphone from the centre circle that Caldey Island Fudge was now available in the club shop.

While at the same fixture, the crew of the *Catrin-Mae* enjoyed the first game of their ten-year ownership of an executive box at the Stadium. As the 'Official Fishing Boat of the Sailors', it was thought only proper they should be able to attend every game for the next decade.

In the second half of the fixture against Ulster, 'What Shall We Do with the Drunken Sailors?' was heard from the crowd for the first time. It quickly became an unofficial anthem of the club.

This was the club that the 17-year-old Gethin Hughes was joining.

"I was really chuffed to have been offered the contract at the Sailors. They were my local team, I'd been to see them quite a few times, and knew some of the boys there already from age-group level. Also, just before signing I'd seen the kit for the new season. It was well smart – lovely flashes of white and black plus the big yellow lighthouse – proper stuff. Some of the lads thought it was silly, but I thought I'd look great in it and couldn't wait to get it on."

Gethin became a Sailor alongside four other local prospects who'd been added to the full squad from the Academy – Matthew Lovering, Rob Price, Alex Anderson and Aki

Loven. Also joining were newly signed Welsh internationals Chris Norwood and Tomos Maunder, and the international acquisitions, Moldovan Ion Ungureanu, American Zac Holt and the star signing of the summer, Australian Niles Turner.

All new members of the Sailors squad, even if like Gethin they'd probably be playing most of the year in the Academy, have to take part in an initiation ceremony. Whether a seasoned international or Gethin Hughes from up the road in Maes-y-Tawe, it has to be done.

A week before pre-season began, the whole squad assembled at captain Lewis Smith's house for a barbeque. Smith had replaced Owen Rhys, who had been abruptly stripped of the captaincy mid-season in 2009, for reasons nothing to do with the Caldey incident, and the 62-capped Wales lock was widely viewed as a good influence on the squad. We let him share the details of his first meeting with Gethin:

"I'd heard about this kid and his potential before he'd signed. We were losing a lot of prospects to Criccieth so it was a bit of a statement when we got him. So, we were having the traditional barbeque at my place and all the new boys were there. We'd had a few beers, but not too much – didn't want any of that nonsense starting back up again – and it was time for the initiation. Nothing too crazy. I know some rugby clubs still did the old-school initiations: the 'Dutch Manager', the 'Silken Glove', the 'Bosnian Bandit'. I even heard about one Scottish club making the boys do a 'Soggy Pringle', but we weren't about that any more. This year it was standing on a chair and singing a song.

The lads were all ticking along – bit of 'Wonderwall', 'Don't Stop Believin'' and the like, and a couple of them were pretty

good, actually. Then came Gethin. He'd been pretty quiet, I
think – bit shy, like. He was still a kid, after all. But he stood up
on a chair and he started doing the Macarena, all the moves,
the arms on the shoulders and everything – the works. He'd
even learnt the original Spanish lyrics. The lads absolutely
cracked up. It was actually pretty impressive in a mad way.
When he finished, he just got down off the chair and sat down.
So yeah, that was how Gethin announced himself to the squad.
We thought then we had a bit of a character on our hands."

The season began with Gethin playing midweek games for
the Development Squad, and he quickly established himself
as a confident player – scoring six tries in his first four
games. He was now playing at a far higher standard than
he had at Maes-y-Tawe RFC or in school, but was clearly
thriving. Matt Draper was Academy Director at the Sailors
during this time:

"I would never have said it at the time, and certainly not to him,
but he found the step up to Academy rugby pretty easy. We
are about two things really: identifying talent and then creating
a pathway to success. Myself and the other coaches all hope
that that success will be with us, but we acknowledge that it
might be with other clubs or indeed in their non-rugby life.
Most of the boys don't make it as professionals. But I remember
watching his first training session and even though he was a
year younger than most of other boys, it was pretty clear he'd
make it. He was as comfortable in attack as he was in defence.
With the ball in hand he was pretty deadly, he regularly scored
tries and had begun to bring kicking into his game too. His
movement was fantastic. He didn't run. He glided. On his first
Academy game, against Cardiff, he scored a try from his own
half – all his own work. From the moment I saw him, I knew we
had something special. Trouble is, he knew it too. He wasn't

short on confidence on or off the pitch, and yes, this did rub a
few of the boys up the wrong way."

At the time that Gethin was welcomed into the club, the
Sailors had just appointed a new manager. Geert van Binder,
the 6' 6" World Cup-winning South African, was brought in
with two clear aims: clear out any bad eggs from the Sailors
squad, and finally win some silverware.

The Sailors had begun the 2009/10 season poorly. Van
Binder had given a chance to some of the veterans he'd
inherited, but just three wins from eight games led him
to look for a change. He'd watched most of the Academy
games since joining, and Gethin along with hooker Matthew
Lovering had caught his eye and were added to the squad
for the away fixture at Newport against the Borderers.

The league that Gethin would make his debut in was
the short-lived Yorkshire-Ireland-Wales-Scotland-Italy-
Cornwall Championship. The result of a struggling Celtic
League and one of the regular English rugby civil wars, the
league operated for two years and was divided into a pair
of regional conferences.

As you'll remember, it never really took off. Zebre versus
Cornish Pirates or Connaught versus Leeds Carnegie
didn't capture the imagination of rugby fans. The first few
months of the championship were also overshadowed by
a legal battle with Irish cider producer, Monahan's, who
signed a sponsorship deal before it was agreed the league
would be known by the acronym YIWSIC. A brand looking
to shake off the dubious reputation of cider weren't happy
about the league's official tagline being the 'The YIWSIC
Championship brought to you by Monahan's Cider'.

Arguments about the sponsorship of the league were
of no interest to Gethin. He was now balancing his time

between Academy rugby and A Levels, studying English Literature, Archaeology and PE at Maes-y-Tawe College. And excelling across the board. His Archaeology lecturer, Gideon Masters, gave us some insight into Gethin the student:

"In all my years teaching this subject, I've never taught anyone quite like young Gethin. I'm no fan of the sporting life, so didn't know he was a player of such a high standard – aside from his fondness for tracksuits and the occasional black eye or split lip, you'd never guess he was rugby man. Though perhaps I should have guessed when he submitted an essay comparing the decline of Roman rule in Cambria – or Wales, as it's known now – with that of the national rugby team in the 1980s. He quite convincingly argued that hubris, a lack of investment and the Northern English were to blame for both collapses. I had to ask one of the PE teachers if this were true – he read the essay and after i explained what some of the longer words meant to him, he agreed. Gethin was quite a remarkable fellow, even at that age."

Putting his studies aside on the day of his debut, Gethin started on the bench. However, a 12-3 deficit at half time saw him replace starting outside centre, Welsh international Morgan Green. It was a proud moment for the Hughes family, with his mum, dad, brother and younger sister in the Rodney Parade stands. Someone who had preferred skateboarding and English literature to rugby for most of his teenage years was now making his debut in a televised Welsh derby.

Geert van Binder was already under a little bit of pressure by the time Gethin first took the field in a Sailors shirt. A well-known and respected figure in the game, with a World

Cup Winners medal won in 1996, he had struggled in recent years to find a long-term coaching role, bouncing around between his native South Africa, England and Japan. He hoped that in South Wales he would find some stability and success. But results had been poor, the new players had – aside from Ion Ungureanu and Tomos Maunder – not performed as expected and Niles Turner, the Australian star brought in to spark the back line, had been inconsistent amid rumours of homesickness.

It was Turner who would line up in midfield with Hughes that day, and though now back on the Gold Coast, he remembers that day well:

"Yeah, I didn't have the best start to playing in Wales. I thought it was going to be fun, but it was raining all the time, the team wasn't really clicking and my missus dumped me over Skype a week after I got out there – I was pretty devo about that. Anyway, that day we were playing the Borderers, it was pretty flat and then Huge came on. I'd seen him do the Macarena at the barbie and laughed a lot, and watched a few Academy games and he looked okay. But didn't really know much more until me and him were at 12 and 13. First couple of minutes he was pretty quiet, then all of sudden he slipped a tackle, went round a couple of guys and put Maunds [Tomos Maunder] away in the corner. Pretty nice.

We picked it up but were still behind. We had a scrum and he started shouting at me to swap positions – I told him to piss off at first, this comes from the captain. But he kept going. Real persistent. With a few minutes to go, we had another scrum and he kept shouting 'swap, swap'. So I just thought: well, we are losing – if that's what the kid wants, let him do it. So we did swap, he got the ball straight outta 10 and obviously fancied their 13 as he just went right through him on an angle, clipped round the Fully and went under the posts. He'd won us the game. I thought it was pretty cocky ordering me around, but fair dinkum, he'd got us the W."

The Sailors had beaten the Borderers in Newport 15-12 and Gethin had been the difference. With the game being shown on BBC Wales, it was the first time that the rugby public had seen what he was capable of and it would be the beginning of a fantastic season for him.

In the next game, versus Cornish Pirates, he again started on the bench, but this time came on in the first half as an injury substitute and scored a try in another Sailors win. He would start the next game and in the course of one month moved from Academy player to first team regular. For the first time the press began to pay attention to him, a feature about him appeared in the *South Wales Evening Post*, *Scrum V* put together a short montage of some key moments in recent games and Gethin started his own Twitter account, @GethinHughes92.

@GethinHughes92

Going to give this Twitter thing a go then. Let's see how it goes.

Retweets 1 Likes 2

For much of this debut season at the Sailors he was still just 17, and his youth caused a problem for the BBC after one game, recalls veteran journalist Aneurin Reeves:

"I've been fortunate to have played, coached and broadcast about rugby football for over 50 years and Gethin Hughes was one of the finest Welshmen I ever had the pleasure of seeing play the game. I know that is an unpopular opinion now, considering all that happened to him, but I maintain it.

He was a fantastic player, his movement was sublime and his confidence at such a young age was remarkable.

I believe it was a game against Munster, away at Thormond Park at Christmas 2009, when he won Man of the Match. I was conducting the interview with young Gethin and had handed him the customary bottle of champagne. We are live on air when suddenly the producer in my ear's yelling 'take it back, take it back!' I carry on the interview, asking him about the game and his performance – he's still pretty shy at this stage – but the shouting continues: 'He's only 17, he can't drink!' At that point one of my BBC colleagues arrives, sweating and wide-eyed, with a small bottle of sports drink and says give him that instead. Personally I didn't see anything wrong with him getting the champagne, but rules are rules, I guess. It was a bit awkward swapping the bottles with him live on air, but I understand the clip proved quite popular on the world wide web, and we all had a good chuckle about it later on."

Re-watching the video now, it's striking just how shy Gethin is when on camera. His Sailors jersey seems too big for him, almost like he's borrowing his dad's for the day. The answers to Reeves' questions are short and spoken in a quiet tone, and he struggles to make eye contact. His blond hair is gelled down across his forehead, almost covering his eyes. And the moment when his bottle of Special Cuvée Champagne is prised out of his hand to be replaced by 500 ml of Lucozade is still an awkwardly amusing moment. Gethin meekly stating, "but I was going to give that to my mum, like I did after the Ystradcarew game," added a layer of pathos and helped this clip get over one million YouTube views. It was even shown on ESPN *Sportcenter* – America's most popular sports show – where his name was pronounced 'Get-hin', much to his teammates' amusement.

After a poor start, the 2009/10 season turned out to be

one of promise, with several of the other Academy players joining Gethin as regulars in the match-day squad. Trophies still eluded the Sailors, with them finishing third in the league and not progressing beyond the quarter finals of the European Shield, but the team had evolved over the course of the season and hopes were high for further progression in the following season.

Among a string of strong performances in the second half of that season, one in particular stands out: the fixture against Y Gorau in Llanelli. This local derby is always a tight fixture, and so it was on Easter Sunday of that year. With five minutes to go, it was 16-14 to the home side. The Sailors were at the edge of Y Gorau's 22 and although going through the phases, they were failing to make any progress with the ball. It looked like a drop goal was the only way through, but with Sailors outside half Chris Norwood limping, Gethin moved into the pocket. From a ruck, the ball was spun out to him; he shaped with his right foot but the home defence was on him too quickly. Seeing the kick would be charged down, he took the ball back up into his hands and as the first defender was about to connect with his right side, he sidestepped. Moments before being charged into the ground, he dropped the ball onto his left foot, his wrong foot, and connecting cleanly with it, the ball sailed over the posts. He'd won the game.

It was a moment of balletic brilliance in amongst the brutality of a Welsh derby, and one that officially made him a hero to the Sailors fans.

Winning drop goals and Man of the Match performances – just what sort of teammate was Gethin in his debut season? Rob Price, the versatile back row and a fellow Sailors Academy graduate who would eventually follow Gethin into the Wales team, gives us some insight:

"Geth's a good boy, he's a cracking player and we had some great times together. But he can be a bit of a funny one... that first season, he'd normally be pretty quiet in the changing room, then he'd just chirp up and say something. I remember one game, the first half had been pretty dismal and at half-time Geert was giving us a good rinsing. Suddenly Geth put his hand up. Like in school. And then he said, real slow like, 'I think everyone should just give me the ball more.' Some of the boys had to stop a laugh – I just thought, oh shit, he's in for it now. Geert stared at him for a minute, then said, 'Well, maybe the boy's got a point.' I couldn't believe it, Geert was normally a bit of a header when it came to discipline – real Afrikaner, y'know. But he let this slide. Though to be fair, Geth scored a great try that second half, and we won the game. So I guess he was right. Still, some of the boys thought he was a bit too cocky, even then."

Although performances on the pitch were impressive, there was still no guarantee that Hughes would turn professional. Not because of doubts about his ability but due instead to his own interests outside rugby – in particular English literature. He'd been offered a place at the University of East Anglia to study the subject, and as amazing as it might seem to the rugby public, he almost took three years of Thomas Hardy, Sylvia Plath and *Neighbours* twice a day over the Sailors, Wales and the Lions.

"All the boys from home thought I was crazy. I knew I'd get a contract from the Sailors but I was still fancying going to uni. I liked English, the student life looked a laugh and I thought I could still play a bit of rugby there. The club knew I was umming and ahhhing over it. Then one day I get a phone call and it's a guy saying it's Neil Malcolm [Wales Coach]. I think it's a joke – one of the boys, like – so I tell him to piss off and hang up. But he calls back, and I think hang on, this sounds like him. Turns out it was. Seems he'd heard a few good reports about me, and was telling me that I had a great opportunity. Can't remember too much about what he said, but he did tell me I had a 'whole life to read some books' but only a few years to play rugby. So I thought then, yeah, perhaps I should give it a go after all. Sometimes I think back about what would have happened if Malcs hadn't called. Who knows, eh?"

On turning 18, Gethin signed his first professional contract with the Sailors, tying himself to the Swansea region for four years. Present at the signing was Gary Johns, Gethin's new agent and one of Welsh rugby's most controversial figures.

Johns' career was built on a brief burst of fame, when as an amateur he reached the third round of the 1994 World Snooker Championship. It was there that he acquired the nickname 'the potter from Pentre'. And from that he carved out an unlikely career as a local radio DJ (for Radio Red Kite, one of South East Ceredigion's most popular radio stations – slogan: 'Hits Happen'), and sports agent. Johns represented several snooker players, a few rugby professionals and a smattering of minor celebrities. He had been bankrupted twice: in 2003 after investing in a llama farm in New Quay, and again in 2007 after his own 'heritage fashion' range, Cardi Cardigans, collapsed.

Johns has repeatedly declined to contribute to this book but we have been able to solve one of the great riddles of modern sport: why he has represented Hughes for his entire career, despite his teammates all being with major agencies based in Cardiff or London.

Gary Johns is Gethin Hughes's nanna's cousin. And anyone who knows Welsh families will know this is why

Gethin has kept him as his agent, throughout the ups, downs and further downs of his career.

However bad things have got, he doesn't want to upset his nanna.

But for now Gary was only a peripheral figure for Gethin – this first season had been all about the rugby. And the rugby had been good. This first season had been a triumph. He'd begun as a member of the Academy and finished it as regular in the first team, with 18 appearances and 7 tries to his name. He was voted as runner-up in the Wales Rugby Writers Awards 'Breakout' category, behind Capitols number 10, Emyr Glendower Jones-Parry. And he'd received his first international call-up and would be joining the Wales U20 squad for a summer tournament in Canada.

If his first season had been a breakthrough success, his second would define him as perhaps the finest player of his generation.

CHAPTER THREE

Entering the Dragon

"I'd not seen a Welsh player so confident or so skilled
with the ball since the 1970s. If he'd swapped the fake tan
and the gold boots for a moustache and headband, he
would have fitted right into that golden era."

"I would also like to recommend that Gethin Hughes give
greater consideration to what he endorses. His support
of this product has led at least indirectly to over 300 arrests
and nearly 120 hospital admissions."

***

JUNE 2010 SAW Gethin turn 18 and represent his country
for the first time, playing in a triangular U20s tournament
against Canada and Scotland in Montreal. Wales won,
Gethin notching a try in each game and collecting the first
medal of his senior career – the first of three he would win
over the next 12 months. His fortnight in Canada would
also be the first time he'd play alongside several of the key
players with whom he'd share so much success, and then
ultimately acrimony, with the senior Wales team.

One of these was the player of the tournament: Capitols
outside half, Emyr Glendower Jones-Parry. He was a player
first spoken about as a future Wales captain at the age of
12, when he captained his school, Ysgol Gyfun Gymraeg

Llanlewin, to the U16 national championship. A regular in age-group rugby for Wales throughout his teens, he also famously won a gold medal at the National Eisteddfod for his harp playing at only 14, was an international-level show jumper and would shortly be the fourth generation of his family to study medicine.

Gethin, fresh from the Swansea Valleys, at this time still vacillating between shyness and confidence, and Jones-Parry, the Cardiff surgeon's son with the smooth assurance of knowing just what his future held, would between them conjure up some of the Welsh rugby's most recent golden moments. But a moment on that tour put the first crack into the relationship, as recalled by Gethin:

"We'd won the first game, beating Canada, and had been allowed out for a few drinks. And well, basically, we were all pretty young and a bit excited, and we didn't really respect the curfew much. Well, we didn't respect it all, to be honest. Pretty much the whole squad was out. All on the dancefloor of this club, drinking some beers, having a laugh when at about 2 a.m. Nobby walks in [Wales U20 coach Dean Norbert]. He looks furious and he can see we're all pretty hammered. Emyr had been with us, drinking too, but when Nobby arrived, he must have been in the toilet or something so wasn't spotted. Apparently he climbed out the window, as he was back in the hotel by the time we were all dragged back, so the coaches thought he'd been in all night.

That wouldn't have been a big deal, but the following day Emyr actually gave us all a talking to about responsibility and maturity when away with Wales. He really got into it and singled me out, saying stuff about me not respecting traditions and things being different now, that I wasn't in 'Maes-y-wherever' now and I had to step up. I bit my tongue – I was pretty new to all this stuff but thought it was pretty rich as I'd seen him drinking a pint of lager out of a Mountie's hat just a few hours earlier. He was always good to play with but I guess me and him never really recovered from that."

Back from Canada, Gethin started 2010/11 at the same pace he'd finished the previous season. A freshly confident Sailors, buoyed by several new signings including Irish hooker Liam Dowd and Welsh international eight Cerith Clement, were one of the favourites for this year's Celtic League and won every game in September and October. Gethin scored 5 tries in those first eight games, and even took over the kicking in duties in one game, claiming two conversions and a penalty.

With the idea of going to university kicked firmly into touch and the rugby career having started strongly, he moved out of his family home and into a shared house with several of the other young Sailors players in Swansea Marina. For the young Gethin it was a bit of a shock having to now do his own cooking and cleaning, and his first time away from home was not without its mishaps.

Matthew Lovering, a fellow resident in what quickly became known as 'The Animal House', recounted Gethin's first attempt at cooking a pizza, where he placed it in the oven with the polystyrene base still underneath. With the fire alarm going off and acrid black smoke pouring out of the kitchen, a surprised Gethin remained adamant this was how his mum made pizza, even telling the firemen that it must be a problem with the oven.

Kitchen mishaps aside, Gethin's performances on the pitch continued to catch the eye, and he was now for the first time receiving major attention from the Welsh rugby media. The focus was mainly on the fast pace of his move from Academy rugby to first-team regular, and on whether this could be sustained. A factfile in the Sailors' match programme for the game versus Glasgow is a nice illustration of the 18-year-old Gethin:

Full name: Gethin Andrew Hughes

Nickname: Geth or Get Hin after ESPN showed that video last year

Favourite player growing up: Mike Phillips

Hardest opponent: My sister Teleri in Monopoly. In rugby? Aidan Dunn was good for Ulster last year

Favourite food: Mum's pizza

Favourite drink: Milk

Favourite TV series: *Prison Break*

Favourite book: *Not That He Brought Flowers* by R S Thomas

Favourite album: The Killers – *Hot Fuss*

Favourite Sailors moment: Drop goal against Y Gorau last year

Favourite other sport: Skateboarding – not allowed to do it any more!

The week before the Wales squad for the Autumn International series was named, Gethin had been Man of the Match in a 15-12 win over Criccieth, Sailors' first win over the North Walians in five years. A particularly lively performance, it led to some of the Welsh press and BBC rugby magazine show *Scrum V* mentioning Gethin's name in relation to the national team for the first time.

At this point, Wales had a settled centre partnership of Y Gorau's Dafydd Brown and Nick Pratley, with over 90 caps between them, and Wales Coach Neil Malcolm wasn't known for opting for callow youth over experience. But with a number of other options missing through injury, Gethin was called into a Wales senior squad for the first time alongside fellow fresh faces Emyr Glendower Jones-Parry, Matthew Harris and Charlie Bevan.

The step up from Academy to Regional, to U20s and now to full international in just over 12 months was almost complete.

"I was pretty shocked to get the call, to be honest. I knew I was having a good season, but didn't think I'd be playing for the full Wales team anytime soon. So it was pretty crazy when I went to the Vale [the Vale of Glamorgan hotel where the national team trained, nicknamed the 'Jail of Glamorgan' under a previous ultra-strict manager], walked into the team room and it's full of faces from the telly. I was the youngest there, and although I knew what I could do on the pitch, it took a while to sink in. That stupid autograph story didn't help either. I was only getting Dean [Jeffries, captain] to sign a birthday card for my nanna. One of the boys spotted it and everyone had a laugh. That's all there is to it. And to be honest, I got a bit annoyed when I read the story."

The autograph story was one run in *The Sun*:

Please Sir!

WALES STARLET BEGS TEAMMATES FOR AUTOGRAPHS

WALES PROSPECT GETHIN HUGHES brought an autograph book to his first training session with the national team and demanded his new teammates sign it before joining them on the pitch. The 18-year-old Sailors centre, who has lit up the opening months of the season, was, according to a source close to the team, 'begging the Wales team, including captain Dean Jeffries' to sign his book for him...

The autograph story was picked up by a number of other websites and caused a brief buzz on social media – for the first time Gethin had to deal with some negative attention. He didn't make the match-day squads for the wins over Tonga and Argentina and defeat to Australia. With injuries mounting after three physical encounters, he was added to the bench for the last game of the series against New Zealand.

What happened in the 72nd minute of Gethin's first international changed his life. That moment of audacious skill, coupled with the confidence to try it and the ability to execute it – all just two minutes into his first appearance for his country.

Those words of the BBC commentary team again:

"What a moment for young Gethin Hughes. He's proved himself in every game he's played since turning professional, and now he's done it for his country against the very best in the world."

> "Remarkable – what have we got here?"

"Something very special. Something absolutely huge."

What possessed the young Gethin to flick that ball up with his foot whilst grappling with New Zealand full back Noah Ayres?

"I don't know really... I always liked doing keepie-uppies with a rugby ball and as I stretched, I felt the ball by my foot and thought, why not? And I guess it worked."

Why not indeed?

Wales may have lost the game, but Gethin was now hot property. He was the first person requested for post-match interviews, joined the press conference alongside captain Dean Jeffries, and was the subject of the headlines across the newspapers the following day:

Teenage Kicks! 18-year-old Hughes scores incredible try on debut

FLICK OF THE LIGHT
Hughes' wonder try electrifies debut defeat

Sign of the times!
Autograph boy Hughes writes his name in Welsh rugby history

Following on from the BBC commentary, 'Huge' was adopted as his nickname by teammates, fans and even some sections of the media.

From that try to the end of the season for region and country, it's no exaggeration to say that everything Gethin did on the pitch worked. Each gap was found, every pass reached its hands, missed tackles were an exception and the tries kept on coming. Now, at 18, he was able to claim his Man of the Match champagne and soon was able to boast a solid collection of bottles.

He was the starting outside centre for Wales in that season's Six Nations, and had been superb in the first three wins over France, Italy and Scotland. In what was widely viewed as a Grand Slam decider, Wales travelled to Twickenham to face an England team who had also won all three of their matches so far.

With Wales winning 15-12 with six minutes to go, and Wales wing Tomos Maunder in the sin bin for a deliberate knock-on, the away team were coming under some serious pressure.

England were at the edge of the 22 when the ball was spun out to Ed Maisie, the 6' 4" superstar of the England team. On a superb angle, he drove through Dafydd Brown, rounded Dan Smith and was heading seemingly unopposed for the corner.

Seven metres from the try line, as Maisie shaped to put the ball down and a small smile began to emerge on his face, running hard from the side was Huge.

He knew he had to hit Maisie with everything he had if he was to stop a match-winning try.

The game, and the championship, would come down to this moment.

Leaving the ground, he propelled himself into Maisie's ankles at the moment he dived for the try line, forcing them towards the touchline as the ball was being grounded.

The Twickenham crowd erupted and Maisie leapt up roaring and slapping the red rose on his chest.

However many times the video is re-watched, Huge's reaction is still astounding.

Getting up a touch gingerly, he stands up, looks across at the celebrating Maisie and slowly raises his right hand and begins to wag his index finger. Stony faced and immune to the jeers of the white-clad crowd just behind him, he then begins to shake his head solemnly. Gethin looks for all the world like a student teacher trying his best to tell off a particularly naughty pupil.

Maisie grins at him, winks and begins to jog back up the pitch before spotting the referee indicating to the

Television Match Official that he'd like him to review the try. A glimmer of concern appears across Maisie's face.

Two agonizing minutes and numerous replays follow.

The 'heartbeat' sound is played over the PA system.

Huge is back with the Wales players, shaking his head, telling them to calm down.

No one in the stadium knows what will happen next.

Except for Gethin.

He knows.

"No try."

By the smallest of margins, Gethin has pushed Maisie's giant size-14 left boot off the pitch, touching the whitewash the briefest of moments before he grounds the ball.

The groans and frustrated shouts echo around the stadium – bar the pockets of red, who go ballistic.

Huge has saved the day. Wales win the game 15-12.

One of those who Maisie had eluded on his way to the line was Y Gorau centre Dafydd Brown, who remembers that moment well:

"I really owed Huge for that. I'd lost Maisie in the tackle and thought he'd won the game for England. I remember scrunching up my eyes in frustration as he went over the line. I knew I'd be in for it in the press and on Twitter. Then I open them and I can see Huge wagging his finger and shaking his head. The England players are going crazy but he jogs over to me and says, 'Don't worry, I got him.' No one seemed that confident when the TMO was up but he kept repeating over and over, 'Don't worry, boys, I got him.' Fair play, I think this was like his fifth cap and he certainly wasn't short of confidence. And yeah, he got him. Hell of a tackle."

The newspapers the following day all led with the image of Gethin wagging his finger at the giant smiling Maisie. A few columnists wrote that it was unsporting, others that he should have shown more respect to his opponent. *Daily Mail* columnist Tobias Cooke was most stinging in his criticism:

> "This kind of cheap gamesmanship has no place in rugby, particularly in front of the game's most intelligent and knowledgeable fans at HQ. This may play well in the Labour-voting heartlands where Hughes 'was raised' but if he wishes to engage in these kind of public stunts then he should play soccer. Rugby is not a game for this kind of person and the quicker he learns that, the better…"

But the Welsh fans loved it, calling it the Finger of God in a nod to Diego Maradona's Hand of God from the 1986 football World Cup. Within minutes of the moment happening, memes of Gethin defiantly wagging his finger at King Kong, dinosaurs from Jurassic Park and other massive figures would soon go viral across the internet using the hashtag #HugeWag.

T-shirts of Gethin and Ed Maisie were being sold on the streets of Cardiff by the following Saturday, when Ireland arrived for the final game of that year's tournament. A 26-16 win secured a Grand Slam, with Gethin scoring a fine first-half try – his second of the Championship. He'd started each of the five games, was Man of the Match in three and was named Player of the Tournament with 68% of the vote. He finished ahead of teammate Emyr Glendower Jones-Parry, who had taken over kicking duties during the tournament and finished as its top scorer.

Gethin Hughes was now officially a Welsh rugby superstar.

It had been a whirlwind few months for Gethin, and he was about to be propelled from the sport section to the celebrity pages. Not only would he collect his trophy at the Six Nations Awards but it would also be the night when he would meet Heledd Harte for the first time. He'd had a few girlfriends through school and college, but nothing serious, and nothing to prepare him for 'Wales' girl next door'.

A familiar figure on the Welsh showbiz scene, Heledd Harte first came to prominence with her own YouTube channel, 'Miss Cwtch'. The Brecon native had since presented a series on Welsh teenagers on BBC Wales, hosted a youth-orientated chat show on S4C, released a clothing range designed for sixth formers and when she met Gethin, was recording her debut album. This debut album, entitled *Hartebreaker*, was described by her label as 'a heady mix of pop, R&B, the Mabinogion and the Brecon countryside of Heledd's teenage years...'

The media reported that she made a beeline for Gethin, took a selfie with him and the Player of the Tournament trophy and instantly uploaded it to her Twitter account. They swapped numbers and would go on a first date – bowling – later that week. With the evening carefully chronicled on Instagram and Twitter by Harte, all of Wales knew they were an item before Gethin did.

Some later wondered if both came to that Awards evening to collect a trophy.

With a Six Nations winner's medal, a Player of the Tournament trophy and a pop star as a girlfriend, Gethin returned to the Sailors in March a different proposition to the one that had left in January.

It might be hard now to remember Huge-mania, but between 2011 and 2013 it was a real phenomenon. This handsome, talented and increasingly confident young man seemed to be about to herald in a new golden era of Welsh rugby. The media absolutely loved him: articles about his childhood and interviews with his parents, teachers and friends featured in newspapers and on websites.

The Guardian, excited upon learning of Gethin's love for the late Welsh poet R S Thomas, took him up to the Llŷn Peninsula for a photo shoot and interview at the church where he had served as vicar. The feature, entitled 'The Boy Who Came Out Of The West' – a nod to the R S Thomas biography, *The Man Who Went Into The West* – caused some bemusement amongst his teammates, with the stern image of Gethin standing in a graveyard looking out to sea that accompanied the piece being pinned up in the changing room. But at this stage, Gethin was a slightly eccentric, increasingly confident but supremely talented and effective player.

> **@GethinHughes92**
> The lads have started calling me NASA as I'm so good at putting men in space
> Retweets 3,481 Likes 1,890

Perhaps the best (or should that be worst?) example of Huge-mania was a snap poll posted by Wales' most popular news and sport website, Wales World, in the minutes following the win over England. The question was, 'Who is the Greatest Welshman of all time?' There were ten options and alongside Gethin, voters could have backed Owain Glyndŵr, Roald Dahl, Richard Burton, Aneurin Bevan, David Lloyd George, Shane Williams, Gareth Bale, Gwynfor Evans or Tom Jones.

The final results saw Gethin just edged out by the founder of the National Health Service as the greatest ever Welshman:

WW Sport > Rugby

Who is the Greatest Welshman of all time?

Results of our readers' poll:

1. Aneurin Bevan (36%)
2. Gethin Hughes (34%)
3. Owain Glyndŵr (18%)

No, Huge didn't almost secure an independent Wales in a desperate struggle against the odds, nor did he lay the foundation stones of our National Health Service, but he has just beaten England, electrified the regional rugby scene all season and, although he didn't quite win our poll here, we all agree he looks better with his top off than Aneurin ever did.

Awards like this aside, Gethin had to refocus when back at his region. Although they had been knocked out of the European Cup by Toulon, with six games remaining in the League, they were five points clear at the top. Home wins over Y Gorau and Zebre, followed by a hard-fought win at Munster, meant that beating Connaught would hand them League victory.

In a season of highlights, Gethin perhaps saved the best until last. In a majestic performance in rainy Galway, he scored a hat trick of tries in a 41-11 win, the third of which saw him pick up the ball in his own 22 and weave past three defenders before outsprinting the covering full back to go over in the corner.

Another day, another trophy. The first the Sailors had ever won, and Gethin was once again at the heart of it.

For some he proved a surprise. Geert van Binder:

"My mission, and I thought of it as a mission as it needed military discipline to be successfully executed, was to win a trophy that season. In the August, Hughes wasn't a part of my thinking; by May he was my main man. I've won the World Cup. I know what it takes to win. And by God, did Hughes know how to win that year. I can't fault anything he did. The club owes him a lot."

For others, he fitted into the grand narrative of Welsh rugby. Aneurin Reeves, the veteran BBC broadcaster and journalist:

"That season was a special one, there's no doubt about that. And yes, it's a team game, and Wales were excellent that championship, but there really is one player who brought a magic touch to the game that year – Gethin Hughes. I'd not seen a Welsh player so confident or so skilled with the ball since the 1970s. If he'd swapped the fake tan and the gold boots for a moustache and headband, he would have fitted right into that golden era. And I can't give higher praise than that."

And for Gethin, what did this special season mean to him?

"Looking back, it was all a bit of a blur. I mean a few months earlier, I was still thinking of going to university and packing rugby in. And then I'm playing for the Sailors, with Wales and winning those trophies. Sure, I was working hard in training but to be honest, it was easy. Everything I tried came off. The gaps were there, the passes landed and when I wanted to hit someone, like in the England game, I did. It was great… did I appreciate it? Probably not enough. But it all happened pretty quickly and I was still young. I'd just met Heledd, and I left a lot of the stuff off the pitch to Gary and yeah, I probably shouldn't have."

With continued success on the pitch and his relationship with Heledd Harte giving him a profile beyond just rugby fans, a number of commercial opportunities came Gethin's way. His first deal was to feature in adverts with Yew Tree Dairy (later renamed Dragon Vale Dairy) promoting yoghurts, then came an agreement to be the face (and body) of Welsh clothing shops Fred's Threads, but the most high profile tie-up was with an energy drink manufacturer to make his own range – Huge Bombs.

At this stage, Gethin had very little involvement in commercial agreements, leaving everything in the hands of his agent Gary Johns, but as he admitted, welcoming the cheques that were arriving and significantly boosting his earnings.

The launch of Huge Bombs was, however, an unmitigated disaster.

The idea was to have two different drinks, one designed to be consumed before exercise – #PITCHBOMBS – and the other before a night out – #CLUBBOMBS. The name itself, in an era of terrorist attacks, should have caused the first few doubts, and the manufacturer being об'єднаний Chemicals of Ukraine should also have sounded alarm bells. But Gethin put his face and a quote ('I'm Gethin Hughes, and when I need to explode, I reach for a Huge Bomb') on the cans. The packaging also carried a faux health warning stating that each drink would cause "excess stamina, excitement, mischief and euphoria."

Huge Bombs were officially launched in Cardiff in May, with the #PITCHBOMBS sports version distributed free across the city's playing fields and the party ones to be given out in town later that evening. While they were marketed differently, toxicology reports later showed that both drinks, luminous green and served in 500 ml cans, were in fact exactly the same.

The city's amateur sportsmen and women were the first to suffer the effects of Huge Bombs, on what the media would later call 'Black Saturday'. A record number of red cards and injuries were reported across Cardiff's amateur leagues, with players being described in the exasperated referee reports as being 'manic', 'deranged' and even 'possessed'. One football match was abandoned after corner flags were used as weapons, the first time this had been recorded in the Cardiff girls' U14 league. A rugby match was abandoned after the referee had to send off both linesmen for fighting each other, whilst a lawn bowls match dissolved into a fracas so ugly that riot police had to be called in to quell it.

The carnage would continue on St Mary's Street that night, as promotions girls and guys wearing Gethin masks handed out cans of #CLUBBOMBS to revellers. Saturday night in Cardiff is always lively, but on this particular evening, the effects of Huge Bombs colliding with alcohol and other substances led to the busiest night in South Wales Police history. Over 300 arrests were made over the course of the evening, with the words 'Club bombs', 'Huge bombs' or 'Huge' featuring in over 200 of the police reports. One merrymaker eventually coaxed down from a flagpole in Cardiff Castle reportedly told police officers that "Gethin made me do it", whilst another partygoer was arrested attempting to gain entry to the museum wearing a Gethin mask and claiming, "Huge is a work of art – he should be in there too."

Such was the extent of the chaos that police had to be drafted in from Powys and Gwent and a phone call was reportedly made to the Army barracks in Brecon requesting troops be put on standby if the disturbances continued.

The effects of Huge Bombs dissipate after 12 hours, so all was calm again the following morning. Very fortunate that no one had died as a result of the drinks he'd put his name to, Gethin was publicly reprimanded by the Chief Constable of South Wales Police, Anya Vaughan:

"We are very disappointed and highly concerned at the terrible events we saw across Cardiff over the weekend. Fuelled by Huge Bombs, which our toxicologists have found to contain dangerously high levels of taurine, caffeine, demerera sugar, paprika and onion plus a number of chemical compounds that remain unknown, we saw anti-social behaviour on an unprecedented scale across the capital. We have banned the distribution of the drinks and urge anyone with any unopened cans to pour the contents away immediately, exercising extreme caution so as not to come into contact with the liquid. Although apparently unaware of the ingredients of the drink, I would also like to recommend that Gethin Hughes give greater consideration to what he endorses. His support of this product has led at least indirectly to over 300 arrests and nearly 120 hospital admissions. He is fortunate not to be facing criminal prosecution."

The manufacturer in the Ukraine could not be traced by the authorities, whilst the UK-based distributor received a major fine and was banned from selling drinks for five years. Even after extensive testing at Cardiff University, one of the chemical additives was found to be unknown to science and renamed Hugeium, in dubious honour of Gethin.

To this day, Huge Night, as it became known, remains something of a legend in Cardiff folklore. Rare cans of Huge Bombs can turn up on eBay and sell for over £200, and many Welsh stag-dos are not complete without one of these pieces of memorabilia getting the evening going. There's even a rumour that Iolo Daniels spirited its creator out of Ukraine and into his castle atop Snowdon in order to secure his own steady supply.

All of this proved a major embarrassment for Gethin, who had to publicly apologize for the damage his drinks had done, make a number of donations to police, ambulance and sporting charities and make personal appearances in nearly every pub in Cardiff to try and make amends.

Such was the goodwill from his on-pitch performances that Gethin largely escaped censure for his role in this bizarre and destructive incident. But both the Sailors and the WRU did hold meetings with him to advise on future conduct off the field – and this, of course, wouldn't be the last time such discussions were had.

However, at this point Gethin was the hottest property in Welsh rugby so his personal standing wasn't damaged too much. There was a large section of Wales that thought the energy drinks fiasco was actually pretty funny. And he had another challenge to focus upon: retaining the Six Nations title and gaining a place on the upcoming British and Irish Lions tour to South Africa.

CHAPTER 4

Monster Hunting

"Am I prepared to go to jail to keep Gethin at the club?
Yes. Yes, I am."

"I'll always remember his last words to me that evening:
'You're an idiot, Hughes – now go to sleep.'"

THE GREATEST HONOUR in northern hemisphere rugby, according to those on whom the honour has been bestowed, is to play for the British and Irish Lions. Every four years, a squad of players is selected from Wales, Ireland, Scotland and England to tour one of the big three southern hemisphere rugby countries. And at the end of the 2011/12 season, the Lions would tour South Africa. A favourite parlour game of fans and press alike is to predict the next Lions squad, usually beginning just a few days after the previous tour has finished. And Gethin over the past twelve months had become a name in everyone's squad.

Stung by some of the criticism following the Huge Bombs debacle, he had aimed to keep a low profile over the summer of 2011. A first holiday with Heledd Harte resulted in only a few photos being sold to the press. And he returned to training fit and raring to go, with the clear focus of another successful season with the Sailors and

Wales and then, if things went well, with the Lions.

But as was so often the case with Gethin, things would not go to plan.

"It was my first day back at training after summer. I'd got in early and was catching up with the boys before our first session when the manager called me into the office. I can't remember exactly what he said, but basically that the club was pretty skint and that they'd had an offer they couldn't refuse from Iolo Daniels up at Criccieth and I was going to be sold to them. He said something about some financial difficulties and them having no choice. I couldn't believe it. I was really happy at the Sailors and didn't want to go north to a place with ghosts – bad memories for me. I stormed out. Left the ground and then some of the madness started…"

Sitting stunned in the car park, he tweeted:

@GethinHughes92
Gutted. Club skint so forcing me to go to Criccieth. Don't want to go. Might quit.
Retweets 1,891 Likes 345

By the time he got home, he had over 100 missed calls from teammates, journalists, friends, family and an irate Sailors Communications Director.

"Yeah, my phone went crazy. My head was spinning. I didn't want to leave the Sailors – I was enjoying my rugby there, and the thought of playing for anyone else at that stage was out of the question. I did honestly think about quitting the game, for a bit anyway."

The Sailors were being similarly bombarded by the media and their own angry fans, who just a few hours earlier had been looking forward to starting the season with rugby's hottest new talent in their ranks.

Gethin was yet to sign any contracts, but a tweet from Iolo Daniels inflamed matters further:

> **@Iolo$16bn**
> Money talks, and talent walks. We got 'im. Croeso Huge!
> Retweets 1,878 Likes 3,410

The Sailors quickly responded with a press release:

> "Whilst we understand the disappointment felt by both the Sailors region and our fans, the offer from Criccieth RFC is so substantial as to be one we are unable to decline. The transfer fee received will help solve a number of financial challenges in both the short and long term..."

And Welsh rugby went mad.

Within hours the Sailors Supporters' Club had mobilized their members, and – as it would soon be known – 'The Battle for Huge' had begun. It started first with a barrage of social media aimed at the club, then an online petition (32,013 signatures in the first hour) and plans being made for a protest outside the club.

The Welsh media stoked this up – making it front page news and the lead story on the evening's news bulletins. It was a trending topic on Twitter and the subject of countless debates in offices, pubs and living rooms.

Looking back at the events of that long, hot July of 2011, it seems a world away.

Two incidents in particular summed up the insane levels of support for Gethin staying at the Sailors.

With Gethin formally placed on 'gardening leave' and the Sailors and Criccieth negotiating fees, pre-season rolled on inexorably. The Sailors had a low-key home friendly lined up against Worcester – a game they never completed.

13 minutes into the game, with the match level at 6-6, approximately 40 fans ran onto the pitch and headed directly for the halfway line. Planned to coincide with the minute matching Gethin's shirt number, this was an operation planned with military precision. The 'naughty forty', as they became known, all had handcuffs and used them to chain themselves together before sitting down in the circle in the centre of the pitch. A few had flags with Gethin's face on them, others T-shirts with his nickname on the front.

Two of the protestors then unfurled a giant banner bearing the demand 'Save our Huge', as a few panicky stewards tried to drag them away. As they fought with the neon-jacketed ones, a low hum was heard coming from the lower East stand – a mobility scooter was heading straight for them. Like a tank from World War One, it slowly but relentlessly headed for the centre of the pitch, the protestors arching their arms to allow it pass below them before reforming their circle. The driver then let off a flare, before – as police would later learn – swallowing the key to the scooter, rendering it immovable until the following morning after breakfast.

It's one of the most powerful images of Gethin's career: 40 fans wrestling with stewards and the police, with the smoke of the flare obscuring flags and banners showing his face. The PA announcer desperately called for calm as the fans in the stands cheered and sang Gethin's name. As a backdrop to the furore were his teammates, adopting the universal rugby pose of hands on hips and wry smiles. The slightly fearful Worcester players had already retreated to their changing room.

Match abandoned.

One of the pitch invaders, once they'd finally left, gave an interview to the *South Wales Evening Post*:

"We aren't just going to let Huge go. Gandhi, Martin Luther King and Nelson Mandela all had to fight for what was right, and we are no different. He has to stay. Am I prepared to go to jail to keep Huge at the club? Yes. Yes, I am."

Making headlines that night across the nation, this was the first action from the newly formed Provisional Wing of the Sailors Supporters' Club (PWSSC), who announced on their Twitter account that they were launching "direct action" to keep Gethin at the club, and promised they'd achieve this "by all means necessary".

The week that followed saw banners with Gethin's face unfurled across the region's bridges, cars belonging to the club's directors vandalized and Iolo Daniels' range of wasabi-based snacks boycotted and in some cases set on fire outside supermarkets.

Through all of this, Gethin kept a low profile, staying off Twitter and not attending training, but when the second major incident happened, he had to comment.

"I was in the house one day when the doorbell rang. It was a journalist asking me for a comment on the Jasper Davies situation. I didn't have a clue what she was talking about, so I just slammed the door. About ten minutes later, my mum called and said had I seen the Jasper stuff, but I didn't know what she was on about. So she told me and well, yeah, I felt pretty bad."

Jasper Davies, for those of you who can't remember, was an 11-year-old boy from Neath, with a rare and life-threatening breathing disorder, treatment for which was only available privately in Florida. His family had organized lots of fundraising activities, and had now raised £15,000 – the amount needed to pay for the treatment – and had booked their trip for a few weeks' time.

But now Jasper didn't want to go for his lifesaving operation. He wanted to give the money to Gethin to make him stay at the Sailors.

"I felt pretty bad when I found out. I'd never heard of this kid, but was told he was very ill and had to get this treatment. I didn't need the money at all and just wanted to get it all sorted with the club. Then he turned up outside my house."

Organised by a London tabloid, Jasper, his family, a film crew and several journalists arrived at Gethin's shared house early one morning and brought with them £15,000 in a big sack. The footage of a sleepy-looking Gethin, still in dressing gown and slippers, confronted on his doorstep by a sickly child he'd never met trying to hand him a bag of cash is certainly not a career highlight for anyone involved.

"I was a bit freaked out by it all. Those journalists were there filming me. I wouldn't take the cash so one told me it was the boy's 'dying wish' and that I should. I thought then it was pretty off. I gave him a match shirt and closed the door. What else was I supposed to do? I spoke to Gary [Johns, Gethin's agent] afterwards, and he was pretty cross – he said I should have taken his money as he had a great buy-to-let in Splott that I could have got involved with. I just wanted to get back playing."

The Jasper doorstep incident was splashed across the tabloid's front page the following day – **"Doorn't bother me! Rugby superstar leaves dying child out in the cold"** – but the threatening of a child's health finally hurried along the deciding of Gethin's future.

Under pressure from fans, with the PWSSC destroying the generator providing power to the club's training ground and briefly holding the club secretary's cat hostage before releasing it unharmed, the Jasper Davies incident and most pressingly dismal season ticket and merchandise sales, the Sailors buckled.

Negotiating with their various debtors and the WRU, they rebuilt their finances. Effectively they were building the club around paying for Gethin, but manage it they did. And much to Iolo Daniels' chagrin, they announced that Gethin was staying at the Sailors.

> **@Iolo$16bn**
> Big mistake from all at the Sailors. But most of all from Huge. People don't say no to me.
> Retweets 2,091 Likes 3,891

Jasper Davies would go on to have his operation and fully recover and whilst declining to contribute to this book, told us that he no longer speaks to his parents.

As fate would have it, the Sailors' first fixture of the new season was away at Criccieth. Although a little short on pre-season, Gethin started at 13. In an electric atmosphere, many of the home fans wore sheets in a nod to the ghost rumours that swirled around his failed trial at the club in 2009, and there was a loud chorus of boos and jeers every time he touched the ball.

As always, Criccieth had spent big in the summer, New Zealand's latest superstar centre Nathan N'ao being lured away from the bright lights of Auckland for a spell on the Llŷn Peninsula. And N'ao, on his debut, seemed keen to make a name for himself by giving Gethin some brutal treatment.

A late hit in the third minute set the tone. A slick Sailors move orchestrated by Gethin saw him knocked to the floor by N'ao moments after releasing Niles Turner for the opening try. Then just before half time, Gethin was raked by N'ao's boot whilst on the floor, his studs making a bloody mess of Huge's shirt. Both incidents were somehow missed by the referee and his assistants.

The game was tied at 14-14 with six minutes on the clock when Gethin made the decisive act of the game. With the Sailors inside the Criccieth 22, a move long planned on the training ground swung into operation. Gethin swapped positions with the Sailors number eight at an attacking scrum as the back line fanned out across the pitch. Mirroring the attack, the Criccieth defence did likewise but before they knew it, they were behind.

The ball came to the back of the scrum, Gethin at eight picked it up, gave an outrageous dummy that the defence swallowed hook, line and sinker, and then sprinted through the gap and under the posts. The ball safely grounded, Gethin lifted his head as a big grin spread across his face, only for the extremely hefty Nathan N'ao to land on his back, elbows first. It was as painful a cheap shot as you'll ever see on the pitch.

"I was delighted to have gone over – in such a niggly game and after all the stuff in the summer, it meant a lot to me. Then N'ao just drops right on me. It really hurt. So I turned and started sorta wrestling with him, then all hell broke loose."

The Moldovan, Ion Ungureanu, is the first man in. Famous for his strength, he picks up N'ao off Gethin and hurls him across the grass. Criccieth captain Brendan Thomas then jumps on Ungureanu's back, wrapping his hands round his neck – which is the signal for both teams, substitutes, and the Sailors physio to wade in for a mass brawl right under the posts.

Punches are being thrown, scrum caps are flying into the air and the TV producer has to mute the microphones on account of all the bad language being picked up.

About 30 seconds into the fracas, Gethin crawls on his hands and knees out from between the legs of one of his teammates (who is throttling a Criccieth substitute), stands up, dusts himself down, runs his hand through his hair and ambles over to a stack of energy drinks.

As the fighting continues, Gethin is a few feet away watching, swigging on a drink with one arm cocked and placed on his waist. The only player on either side not involved. One photographer noticed and turned his attention away from the melee and to Gethin looking on.

This classic image – to the left, the angry faces of a rugby brawl; on the right, Gethin sipping from a drink, coolly looking on – is the picture the press use, adding another layer to the legend. It also perhaps shows how detached he sometimes becomes from the team.

@GethinHughes92

Why didn't I get involved in the fight? Have you seen this face?

Retweets 819 Likes 245

The Sailors win the game 21-14, but Criccieth win the suspension battle, seven players to four.

The Six Nations before a Lions tour is always a particularly spicy one, with players keen to do all they can to make sure they are in the squad. Gethin went into the tournament in most people's squads, although not everyone's Test XV, with Ireland's Hugh Lennon and England's Harry Milne also performing well for club and country.

Wales were the defending Grand Slam champions, but hopes of repeating the feat were dashed with a 19-10 defeat at home to England in the opening fixture. Wins over France, where Gethin scored a fine individual try, and Italy reignited the championship but a scrappy defeat in Dublin left Wales with nothing to play for in the final game in Edinburgh, aside from Lions places.

Gethin had not hit the heights of the previous campaign but still proved to be one of Wales' most consistent performers and most popular players with the media. Always requested by journalists to give pre- and post-match comment, and with Heledd Harte always picked out in the crowd by eager TV producers, this tournament cemented his position in the upper echelons of world rugby.

The game against Scotland would bring him even closer to the hearts of the Welsh rugby public, but begin a schism between him and the team's management.

This time it was not energy drinks or Iolo Daniels causing the problems. It was his long-held fascination with the Loch Ness Monster.

With Wales set to play Scotland at 5 p.m. on the Saturday and a brief captain's run on the Friday morning, the Friday afternoon was meant to be a relaxing time for the players. A coffee and a stroll up the Royal Mile was the order of the day for most of the squad.

Gethin, however, had other ideas.

By 1.30 p.m. on Friday, Gethin was in a pre-booked taxi taking him three and a half hours north to Loch Ness. The plan was simple: there by 5 p.m., a quick boat tour of the Loch, then straight back down to Edinburgh and back in the hotel for the 9.30 p.m. curfew and an early night.

"Well, it's a bit of a funny one really. But ever since I was a kid, I've loved the Loch Ness monster. Got bought a cuddly toy when I was a baby so I think that was where it all started, then got a few books on it, and think I've seen every documentary ever made on the monster. I think it's fascinating. So yeah, when I saw how the Scotland game was arranged, I thought why not? Something off the bucket list, and no harm done. Except of course, that it didn't happen the way it was meant to..."

Gethin arrived on time and boarded a tourist boat, HMS *Ness*. It did a loop around the loch three times a day and was on its final trip that day when it ran into difficulties.

"It was great, we were on board learning all about the monster. I'd bought some binoculars special to see if I could see it. Then suddenly there was a big bang to the back of the boat and the engine cut out. A few people screamed. I ran to the stern, what boat people call the back, and looked down. I saw a massive black shape beneath the water. For a second, it seemed it was the monster and he was going to sink the ship. I thought what

79

a shame it was that people would never see me in a Lions jersey. Especially as the new one had just been released that week and I knew I'd look great it in. There was lots of shouting and suddenly I felt quite cold and the water looked very dark. But then I looked a bit closer and saw it was just a log wedged in the propellers. And we began to drift."

Whilst Gethin was the only Welsh squad member on the HMS *Ness*, he certainly wasn't the only Welshman aboard. 42 members of Cryoes RFC were also on the trip, and had spotted Gethin immediately. Steve Mabbutt, their manager, picks up the story.

"We did a bit of a double take at first, but one of the boys went up to chat to him. Huge said he was trying to keep a low profile, but he was in a Welsh tracksuit with 'Hughes' written across the back. He also kept taking selfies. When we hit the log, I have to admit it was a bit scary but then I thought, no – we won't sink, no God is cruel enough to drown Huge. And I was right."

Whilst the immediate danger had passed, the boat drifted listlessly for an hour before being towed back to shore by a local fisherman. By this time Gethin's taxi had left, and the only way back to Edinburgh was on the Cryoes RFC tour bus. Mabutt continues:

"It turned into a bit of a tour classic, to be honest. We all boarded the bus and the slab of cans was being passed around when one of the boys spotted Huge just standing alone in the car park. He looked a bit upset so we stopped the bus and went out to see him. Seemed that his driver had let him down, so we ended up driving him back to Edinburgh."

The journey has gone down in Cryoes legend. Sitting among 42 of the finest players, administrators and fans of the Cynon Valley team, Gethin had no choice but to partake in the activities.

"Fair play, he didn't have any of the beers, but he played the bingo, happily watched Jurassic Park III and was well into the karaoke. He banged out an amazing version of the Macarena, did the moves and everything – the boys had never seen anything like it. By the time we finally arrived back in Edinburgh at about 2 a.m., we were all best friends. He signed a contract I wrote out on the back of a box of crisps that he'd play for us once when he retired. It's framed and up on the club house wall, so I think that makes it legally binding."

It's lights out at 10 p.m. the night before an international. Gethin was creeping back into his room at gone 2 a.m.

"It had been a good laugh coming back with the Cryoes boys, but not ideal preparation. I sneaked past reception and avoided some of the fans in the bar and was chuffed when I got back into my room. I thought I'd got away with it."

Neil Malcolm, whilst having the flinty edge that many New Zealanders have, was typically a genial and relaxed coach, enjoying a normally lighthearted relationship with his players.

Malcolm could afford to do this thanks to the discipline provided by his Forwards Coach, Ross 'Killer' Collier, an ex-All Black tight head and former head of the Wellington police department murder squad. A product of the amateur era, his nickname Killer applied to both his working week and his time on the pitch. The legacy of his time in

Wales still loomed large over the internationals spoken to for this book – one with a particularly tough reputation telling the author in a hushed tone, "I still see him in my nightmares."

Gethin had already had a late night, and it was about to get later.

"I got into the room and went straight into the bathroom. I'd just started putting on my moisturizer when I heard a voice from over by the bed – 'Good evening, Mr Hughes.' I jumped out of my skin. I almost ran for the door, but I thought I recognized the voice. It was Killer. I peeked round the corner and there he was sitting in a chair in total darkness. He'd been waiting for me all night.

It was horrible. I tried to tell him about the Loch Ness Monster and the boat breaking down and having to get the bus back. But he didn't buy it. He thought I'd been drinking. I hadn't, but he didn't believe me. Next thing I knew, he was getting a laptop out, and then this weird metal dome thing. It was a lie detector! He connected me to it and asked all these questions, first about my birthday and who the Prime Minister was then building up to what I'd been doing that night. I answered honestly but he still wasn't convinced. Then he got a breathalyzer out and I had to do that. He did the test three times. I hadn't been drinking – the only thing I'd have tested positive for was loads of Pringles. Eventually he gave up. I'll always remember his last words to me that evening: 'You're an idiot, Hughes – now go to sleep.'"

The following morning Gethin received a knock on the door before breakfast. It was Neil Malcolm, dropping him not just from the team but from the match-day squad.

Despite passing Collier's tests, he had still broken curfew

and pictures of his time on the Cryoes bus had appeared on social media and then in the press soon afterwards. It appeared, incorrectly, that Gethin had been drinking and the team management had no choice but to drop him.

Gethin's place in the team was taken by the Capitols captain James Beynon, with Sailors clubmate Ben Bowen moving onto the bench.

However, as Bowen was warming up, he pulled a hamstring, meaning that Wales were a man short for the bench. With no other fit backs in the squad, Gethin was quickly told to change and joined the match-day squad as the 22nd man. Aware of the media furore over the incident, he was made to sit next to Killer in the stands, as if sitting next to the coaching team's hard man would stop him straying back up to Loch Ness mid-match.

Several groups of Wales fans in the ground had used their hotel bed sheets to make banners – 'Free the Loch Ness One' and 'Huge is Innocent' – and on more than one occasion the cameras picked up the clump of Cryoes players in the stands who, revelling in their brief moment of fame, had sourced several Loch Ness cuddly toys as well as Gethin face masks.

A dour game, watched by Killer and Gethin – looking for all the world like a father and sulky teenage son waiting outside a headmaster's office – only ignited towards the end of the second half. The teams exchanged tries and it was 17-17 with six minutes left when Gethin was thrown on in place of injured Wales outside-half Parry-Jones. With other second-half injuries, Wales had no recognized kicker left on the pitch so were forced into the move. The reluctance was etched on the Wales coaching team's faces as Huge raced onto the field.

Perhaps they could sense what was coming.

In the final minute, with both teams blowing hard, Scotland were pinged for being off their feet at the breakdown and Wales were awarded a penalty 48 metres out. As Wales captain Dean Jeffries debated with Tomos Maunder what to do, Gethin grabbed the ball and pointed to the posts. A few awkward moments ensued before Jeffries shrugged his shoulders and smiled ruefully – after all, a draw wouldn't be so bad.

In truth it could have been 60 metres and it would still have gone over: it was thumped straight and true and bisected the posts as the final whistle blew. Wales had won 20-17 and Huge had gone from zero to hero in the course of an afternoon.

The Wales team erupted as the kick was successful and they followed Gethin as he hurdled the advertising hoardings, ran up two flights of concrete steps, turned right and jumped straight into the arms of his new friends from Cryoes RFC. Beer erupted everywhere as the plumbers, builders and teachers of this Valleys team celebrated with the finely honed athletes of the national team high in the stands. As the team trotted back down the stairs, a grinning Huge had a Loch Ness Monster cuddly toy tucked under his arm.

Gethin would receive a further fine for this action and another verbal battering from Killer. But as Aneurin Reeves noted in his weekly column, "What Gethin Hughes did, whilst foolish and even provocative, probably did more than any of the major WRU initiatives to reconnect the national team with grassroots rugby."

The next challenge would be very different – no soft Celtic pitches surrounded by adoring fans. It was time to head to the highveld to face South Africa with the British and Irish Lions: Gethin's biggest challenge to date.

CHAPTER 5

Lion Taming

"He disgraced the good name of Nelson Mandela.
And for that I can never forgive him."

"Trust me, I've walked in on roommates
doing much, much worse on rugby tours."

———————————

WHAT WAS DESCRIBED as the "best prepared and most talented Lions squad ever assembled" ended up on a tour widely viewed as the biggest disaster that northern hemisphere rugby has ever known. The players making up a Lions squad are deemed to be the best of the best, and are sent on the last remaining 'full' international tour, taking on clubs as well as a country. Gethin was deserving of his place, and fully expected to make a massive impact in South Africa. But his presence on the tour ended up being remembered for an entirely unexpected reason.

"Of course it's amazing to be picked. That day at the Sailors HQ, sitting round after training watching Sky Sports News and seeing my name called along with so many others, was a real buzz. I think there were six from the region and twelve in total from Wales, so good representation. I was looking forward to meeting the Irish, English and Scottish lads too. Certainly a few of the picks were a bit odd. But I didn't think too much of it at the time. I knew Mands had a bit of a reputation but I just wanted to get down there and show what I could do."

Mands is Pat Mandeville, the Lions Head Coach for the tour. The story of Gethin's tour to South Africa can't be told without revisiting his appointment.

Initially the bookies' favourite was England coach Paul Houghton, but after several meetings he ultimately declined, wanting to focus on his job at Twickenham. Wales coach Malcolm was approached but also turned down the offer, as did Dan Weir, the new man at Scotland's helm. The Ireland coach, Des Hammersmith, initially accepted but then backed out, citing personal reasons. Several club coaches were sounded out, but no luck. With four months to go until the tour, there was no Lions Head Coach.

One man that was available, and had made his thoughts on what success on tour would look like ("winning every game, most by 20+ points") very vocal, was Pat Mandeville. Assistant coach to his native Australia when they won the 2001 Rugby World Cup, he had had spells to mixed success with Harlequins in London, the Capitols in Cardiff and several Super Rugby teams. A larger-than-life character, even at 56 he was famous for wearing shorts whatever the weather. He was known as a strong-man motivator, but had fallen out with key players throughout his career.

His first meeting with his players made a big impact, particularly on Ciarán O'Donnell, the Irish number eight who was on his second Lions tour:

"So all the lads are in the team room chatting away – real good buzz, all in our new stash. Great stuff. Then Mands comes out and starts talking. It took a while for us to properly realize but he was speaking in what seemed like an Irish accent. A pretty poor one at that too. The lads are all looking round making faces. I thought, is he drunk? He starts to tell us that he's coached and lived in England and Wales so feels part of those nations, and that his great-grandfather was from County Meath and he's called Pat so he's Irish too. We laughed at that. And then some guy appears, must be about 17, looking proper sheepish. We were told he's called Hamish, and he's Mandeville's daughter's boyfriend, which makes him Scottish too.

The lads are cracking up at this point. Then he gets his Australian passport out and sets it on fire. He's waving it around shouting about his new country being Lionsland or something, when it starts to burn his hand. He screams and chucks it in a bin and then that goes up in flames. The fire alarm starts to go crazy and the sprinklers are set off. Full-scale emergency evacuation of the hotel. The press were taking photos of us standing in the car park looking like lemons. So yeah, that's how we met Mands and it was pretty much downhill from there."

The 44-man squad selected – 12 Welsh, 14 English, 13 Irish and 5 Scots – had ruffled quite a few feathers. Against expectations, Ireland's veteran fly half Ross O'Carroll Kelly had not been given the chance to make his fifth Lions tour, and England's talismanic hooker Nicholas Putney had also failed to make the cut. Whilst Brad Rennie, an Australian who had never visited the UK or Ireland, let alone played there, was selected on account of a grandmother from Leamington Spa.

First up was a team-bonding weekend in the Shetland Islands that saw three of the team treated for exposure. This was followed by a week's training in Northern Ireland that included a 'Troubles tour' of Derry, resulting in the police having to extricate the squad from a housing estate none too keen on their largely British visitors. Finally a few days in Bristol saw an impromptu jog across the Clifton Suspension Bridge cause traffic chaos. Three tour-ending injuries were incurred during these ten days and the squad was creaking a little before it even arrived in South Africa.

> "It was kind of an odd preparation. We spent a lot of time doing gimmicky things and there wasn't a lot of training, but when we did some it was crazy intense. Pat also gave a lot of lectures, not always about rugby. He did one about stamps, I think something on Princess Diana and another about Irish history which didn't seem to go down too well with some of their boys. I was getting on well with most of the lads, though Emyr [Glendower Jones-Parry] was always getting on my back about stuff. He was locked in to start at number 10, and referred to himself a few times as Simba, 'cos he said he was the Lion King. The Wales boys used to roll their eyes, but some of the English lads loved him – he ended up spending most of his time with them in the end."

Gethin started the first game, against a President's XV in Durban, and notched a try in his 50 minutes on the pitch in a 39-5 victory over largely amateur opposition. It was a nice way to announce his time in a Lions shirt, intercepting a flat pass in his own 22 and scampering straight down the middle before arcing around the full back to go over in the corner. This fine solo effort brought the biggest cheer of the game, due in part to the 40 members of Maes-y-Tawe RFC in the crowd. A photo of Gethin posing post-match, still in his kit, with these boys and their special 'Maes Lions' flag is prominent in their Swansea Valley club house. The image is also up on the wall in the kitchen of Gethin's small flat in Splott, one of only a few reminders of his career that can be seen there.

A comfortable win over Western Cape and a narrow win against the Marauders, which saw Gethin impress in a 20-minute second-half appearance, gave the tour a sheen of promise heading into tougher games. But despite three wins to start the tour, cracks were already appearing.

The tour captain was supposedly English lock Nathan Darlow, who was on his third tour. In his book about the tour, *Lion Man No More*, he makes it clear that this was not really the case:

"We'd just beaten the Marauders after playing pretty well, and Pat called me in. He told me that I was going to stay his captain but that other players would now be his brains, his heart and his knees. I was a bit taken aback. I asked him what that meant, and he said that he'd looked at Minerva and that I couldn't get him the numbers he needed. Again, I asked him what that meant. He said the numbers didn't lie and that I was a .87 in a world where he needed .91. For the final time I asked what that meant, and he said again the numbers didn't lie. I walked out of the room. I stayed captain but I didn't have a one-to-one again with him on that tour. It was a joke."

Minerva was an artificial intelligence programme that the Official IT partners of the tour, LEBAUM, had developed as a bit of marketing fun to support their involvement, giving data on players, metres covered etc. But at some point during the tour, Mandeville seemed to fall under its spell.

Here's Ciarán O'Donnell, speaking to the author at the launch of his book, *Pride No More: An Irishman abroad*:

"Minerva? Aww, jeez – yeah, that thing. It ended up dominating the tour. I think it made all the decisions for Mandeville by the end of it. I remember during one team meeting towards the end of the tour, someone had obviously fiddled with it, and among the squad members displayed on the big screen were Wayne Rooney and Rihanna. Think she was the best-performing forward we had. I'm not sure he even noticed."

Observer rugby correspondent John Telfer, who was in South Africa throughout, noted some more of the quirks of Mandeville's coaching in his book about the tour, *Lions Led By A Donkey*:

"At first glance, the training was of the usual high intensity you would imagine. The players were on the whole working on everything you'd expect and looked to be responding well. Mandeville had some excellent and experienced lieutenants who typically ran the start of the sessions for him. The first hour was fine. It was the second that was odd. The players were divided into groups to work on certain skills. But there was no link between them – they were all jumbled up. Props were working with wingers, locks with full backs. The more we looked at it, the less it made sense. It was always a mystery. We'd always try and get an explanation from the players or coaches but they always just smiled and rolled their eyes, and said it was something the Coach wanted.

The press corps couldn't crack it and the players were all on a Twitter ban, so nothing was coming out from them. It was only after that first Test defeat at Newlands that that we ended up in the hotel bar with Neil Havers, the team doctor. It was a tough afternoon and we'd all had a couple of drinks. Someone asked him about the training groups – we expected the normal stonewalling but then he looked at us and smiled and said, 'star signs'. That is what these players had in common."

Unbeknownst to the Lions committee who had selected him as Head Coach, Pat Mandeville had for several years been in thrall to the power of astrology. He used it for all aspects of his life, and this included team selection. For Mandeville, Taurus and Gemini made the best players, Libra and Cancer the worst. A goal kicker should ideally be a Sagittarius. The captain should never be a Capricorn.

Gethin, a Gemini, came near the top of Mandeville's reckoning and had settled well into what was an often strained camp.

But what type of tourist was Gethin? England second row Billy Eddershaw, on his second Lions tour, was selected as Gethin's roommate, and writes about meeting Gethin properly for the first time in his book about the tour, *In the Lions Pack: My Summer in South Africa.*

"I'd played against him and he was obviously a top player, but he also seemed a bit of a character with the finger wagging thing at Twickenham. Whilst I didn't mind it, he annoyed a fair few of the English lads. So I didn't know what to expect.

Firstly, he had loads of stuff with him. We get given a ton so don't need that much, but he had bags of it. A lot of it seemed to be hair gel! He had about six different types – a training one, a night out one, one for matches and so on.

One night I came back to the room a bit earlier than planned and heard this sort of banging and grunting coming from the room. I thought he might have a girl back there, but I needed to get my charger so I knocked loudly and came in anyway. There he was in the middle of the room with a bloody skateboard. He'd built some jumps and was really going at it. It turns out he's really into that stuff, and apparently he's not allowed to do it any more so does it on the quiet, or in disguise. He swore me to secrecy. So sorry, Gethin! But trust me, I've walked in on roommates doing much, much worse on rugby tours."

Further victories were picked up against the Diamonds, where Gethin played the first 60 minutes, and the Marlins, before a trip to Robben Island and a few days' rest before the serious games got underway.

The trip to Robben Island, the prison island to the north of Cape Town where Nelson Mandela was imprisoned for 18 years, was meant to bring the team together and give the tour – only the second since the end of apartheid – some perspective on the history of South Africa. Instead it saw Gethin caught up in a diplomatic incident, which he explains here in full for the first time:

"So, the whole squad went to Robben Island. We'd gone over on the ferry, and did the full tour – finishing up seeing Nelson Mandela's cell. It was a really interesting day. It's great being on these tours and getting the opportunity to see stuff that you wouldn't normally. Anyway, all good – we get back to the hotel and head straight into dinner. I put my backpack down by my feet and suddenly I can feel it moving. I'm like, what the hell is this? It then starts to slowly move along the floor. All the boys can see it now and are laughing. So I very gently begin to unzip it, with no idea what was inside."

Robben Island is home to a colony of African penguins also known as the jackass or black-footed penguin. And it was one of these penguins that Gethin had in his bag.

"I opened it up and this head popped out. It was a bloody penguin. All the boys were cracking up and Emyr was filming it all on his phone. It then hopped out and started waddling across the floor. I didn't know what to do. Then our liaison officer, Henk, started screaming at me in Afrikaans and it all went a bit crazy."

The commotion in the dining room attracted the attention of several journalists, who managed to catch the spectacle of Gethin chasing a small penguin across the floor of a Cape Town hotel on film. Within minutes the images and video were on Twitter and the story went viral. People all over the world, even non-rugby fans with no idea who Gethin was, watched, liked, commented and shared the video. The press naturally lapped it all up, and the fact that he was Heledd Harte's boyfriend only added to the coverage:

WADDLE AN IDIOT!

On the Robben!
The Welsh legend and Nelson's penguin

Mandela grandson blasts
p-p-pick up a penguin Lion

NOT **Fans react to penguin**
COOL! **theft from Nelson's Island**

Who placed the penguin in Gethin's bag has never been proved. There are many who think it was Gethin himself, but he is adamant it wasn't him.

"The first time I saw that penguin was when its head popped out of the bag. Honestly. We were taken past them on the tour, and a few of the boys stopped for photos with them but I didn't. Plus my bag was on the bus. It wasn't me. Who was it, then? Well, I'm not sure. But Emyr's video went on his Twitter straight away. He never stopped banging on about what a disgrace it was. He even said that I'd disrespected the spirit of

Nelson Mandela. Or Madiba, as he called him – he'd learnt the local name for him and insisted on calling him that instead."

The players' disciplinary committee, presided over by England hooker Tim Lewis – complete with gown, wig and gavel – didn't, however, find him guilty. They instead recorded an 'open verdict', though insisted that Gethin serve the teas and coffees dressed as a French maid during the breakfasts that week, a sentence he begrudgingly but efficiently carried out.

Pat Mandeville had different ideas. Despite Gethin's claims of innocence, he was suspended for 14 days from all Lions activities and fined £10,000. Aside from being absent from the fixtures against the Emerging Springboks, the Dukes and the first Test against South Africa, he also had to return to Robben Island to offer an apology.

The South African press were outraged about what they saw not only as a criminal act, but one that had taken place in one of the most important and politically sensitive places in the country. Whilst the police, after speaking to Gethin, declined to take the issue further, the South African government made an official complaint to the British High Commissioner in Pretoria. There were threats of protests and disruptions at any games involving Gethin. And of course, his Twitter account came in for some serious abuse.

In an effort to defuse the situation, it was decided that Gethin should return to the island on his own, to apologise in person for what had happened.

"I didn't do it. I never saw that bloody penguin before I opened my bag. But I was told that I'd be kicked off the whole tour if I didn't go back and apologise. I called Malcs [Wales Manager] and he told me to do it, as did Gary [Johns, agent], Heledd and my mum so I thought what the hell, everyone thinks I did it so I might as well bite the bullet and get it over with. There were loads of press with me, and I didn't mind seeing the fellas that worked there. But the thing with the penguin was ridiculous."

The Powers That Be decided that Gethin also had to apologise to the penguin.

Re-watching the video of this still brings back a cold sweat for Gethin. But for anyone else, it can't help but force a laugh. Even in a career blighted by absurd moments, this has to be one of the most ridiculous.

For those who need a reminder of the ceremony, Gethin is standing in front of the penguin colony, next to the director of the island, as one of the island's wildlife rangers comes over holding the penguin. He places it down in front of Gethin and the tiny bird begins to waddle towards him.

The assembled journalists and photographers cheer.

Gethin kneels down and says quietly, "I'm sorry."

One of the journalists shouts, "Say it like you mean it."

Gethin repeats his apology a little louder.

"We can't hear you."

Gethin says it again. Louder again.

Then the director of the park leans over and gives Gethin a card. As there are eleven official languages in South Africa and no one can be sure what language the penguin speaks, it's deemed only correct that the apology is also made in Afrikaans, Ndebele, Northern Sotho, Sotho, Swazi, Tsonga, Tswana, Venda, Xhosa and Zulu.

Gethin in his full Lions blazer, shirt and tie, then spends the next 15 minutes apologizing to an increasingly uninterested penguin in a variety of languages written out phonetically for him. Each met with a loud cheer by the assembled press corp and a stern nod from the director when he finally gets the pronunciation right.

After this humiliation, Gethin is given a lifetime ban from Robben Island, a copy of *Long Walk to Freedom* ("to think about real suffering on this island") and allowed to return to the hotel.

> "It was pretty excruciating. It felt like I was there for an age. Some of those words are so hard. I mean Xhosa for 'I am sorry' is 'Ndiyaxolisa'! It took me sixteen goes to pronounce it in a way acceptable to the director. But perhaps I was lucky – the boys in that first Test probably got more embarrassed that week."

The Lions lost that first Test 38-10. With an eccentric team selection, featuring players who had barely played on the tour and several playing out of position, they were never in the game. The second Test was only marginally better, with South Africa winning 25-6 and taking the series.

By the time the third Test rolled around, Gethin's ban had expired and the press' attention was now firmly on the chaos surrounding the squad rather than the penguin incident. Nine players had had to withdraw with injury and three players had walked out of the squad after bust-ups with the coach.

Gethin's Sailors teammate Alex Anderson was on strike after being chastised in a team meeting because of his Minerva numbers in the second Test. The problem was he'd been injured and not played a minute in that match.

Discipline in the squad had collapsed in that final week, with many openly drinking with fans in the evenings. The Scottish players, underused throughout the tour, skipped training en-masse one day and went to a water park instead. The team management only noticed after they saw pictures in the press the following day. Ireland captain Rory Fitzgerald, one of the few players to emerge with any credit from the first two Tests, had started smoking for the first time since he was 15. Several of the squad left the team hotel to stay with their partners and families. One player who started the second Test reportedly moved into a youth hostel for that last week, sub-letting his hotel room to a fan with the promise of an 'authentic Lions experience', in return for £10,000. Kit and apparel only available to players and staff was found being sold on eBay.

It was into this chaos that Gethin was reintroduced. He started the final Test in Pretoria on the bench, but after England centre Ryan Tovey limped off with 30 minutes to go, he finally gained his Lions Test cap. A patched-up Lions faced a mix-and-match Springboks in the liveliest game of the whole tour. The Lions were 21-15 down with 13 minutes to go when Gethin entered the fray.

He converted two penalties either side of one from South Africa to make it 21-24 with a minute to go. Going hard into the Springbok 22, the Lions were awarded a penalty that if kicked, would square the game and give the series a sheen of respectability.

The TV producers zoomed in on Mandeville in the stands, gesticulating wildly at the posts and shouting through his microphone to take the points. This could be seen on the big screen and Gethin, holding the ball in his hand and talking to Rory Fitzgerald, looked up at it and smiled.

"Yeah, the order was coming down to take the kick. But Rory was like, 'Sod 'im. Go for it.' I looked up and saw there was a bit of a gap on the left-hand side of their defence. I gave the ref the nod and just banged over a massive up-and-under in the corner. They weren't expecting it. But Anyo [Reotola, England

97

wing] was and he leapt up, beat their man and put it down in the corner. We'd won the game. Then the screen flashes up Mands, going nuts like we'd lost. Smashing his microphone on the table, chucking his water bottle at the glass. I popped the kick over and the final whistle went. We'd won 28–24.

He was wild in the changing room, really going crazy. Talking about orders and obedience. Calling me a traitor. Shouting about all the Geminis being against him. In the end TB [Tim Baker, Tour Manager] had to come in, put his arm round him and lead him away. That was that. Never saw him again. We all went out that night and had a big one. But everyone was glad to come home. The tour wasn't what we'd hoped."

Dubbed by the press the 'Tour from Hell' at the time, the steady stream of revelations from players and staff on their return and the 16 books about it written for the Christmas market only further underlined how bad it had been. It would take two further tours before the Lions re-established their position and reputation in the rugby world.

Gethin's own tour was a disappointment, overshadowed by the penguin incident. He played only three games in total, including the final Test – just 134 minutes – and scored 14 points. This was however, enough to make him the player of the series according to Minerva. The trophy (a cup with a plastic Springbok, which in truth looks more like a reindeer you'd find on top of a Christmas cake) currently resides in Gethin's loo.

The tour had, however, for both good and bad reasons, raised Gethin's profile beyond just Wales. And the next season would see Gethin return to concentrate on the Sailors and Wales. But with fame, injury and some extraordinary disputes, this focus he desperately needed would be increasingly hard to find.

CHAPTER 6

Sticks and Stones

"Hughes has been good for us but this is just plain stupidity.
He let himself and his team down very badly today."

"To be honest, the money was crazy and I just went for it.
I guess what happened next wasn't great either."

"SO IT WAS crazy, *ja*! I was in a shop in a castle in Wales. I was
DJing in Bristol the night before. Then I woke up in Wales.
Don't ask how! Crazy, *ja*! Anway, I was in the shop buying those
pencils with rubbers at the end you Welsh love and I heard this
lady singing. And I was like, 'Yes! This is a hit!' So I bought the
CD from the lady. Got my laptop out and made the song. Hit,
hit, hit!"

This is the well-known story of how, whilst Gethin was in
South Africa with the Lions, DJ Tryanus Rex discovered
Heledd Harte in the gift shop of Caerphilly Castle and
created her global mega-hit, *'Hoci a sboncen* (Ibiza Mix)'.

Her fame, previously more or less limited to Wales,
now went global. The song was originally an album track
on *Hartebreaker*, her debut album which had peaked at
118 in the UK charts, and was about her love of PE at
her Monmouth boarding school. Now, with the power of
a Dutch superstar DJ behind it, her vocals were dropped

over a beat, an additional sample of a Stevie Wonder b-side and some bagpipes. The result was a number one hit in 16 countries, from the UK and France to Bolivia and Taiwan.

It was, though, the video that most people remember.

Described by one critic as a "the garish Technicolor fantasy of a Plaid Cymru-obsessed teenage boy", the video saw the 23-year-old Heledd dressed in a 'sexy' version of traditional Welsh costume, complete with black stovepipe hat, shawl, unbuttoned white shirt knotted above her midriff, and mini skirt. Filmed in Bulgaria after no school could be found in Wales that would allow it to be recorded on their premises, it's a fairly blatant rip-off of Britney Spears' 'Hit Me Baby One More Time'. Heledd is parading around the school, winking each time the word *sboncen* is sung, before heading out onto the playing field, where her on-screen boyfriend, in full miner's gear and smeared in coal, is playing rugby. The video ends with Heledd and the boyfriend (who looks not unlike Gethin) skipping off into the sunset through a field of sheep.

Controversial in Wales due to its crudely stereotypical view of the country, it was nonetheless a giant smash on YouTube and music video channels around the world. It made Heledd hot property, and a cast an extra spotlight on Gethin as he returned to rugby.

A post-Lions season is always one where injuries hit hardest, and for Gethin this was certainly the case. Despite relatively little game-time in South Africa, he was allowed back to pre-season late, and then missed the first month of matches with a calf injury. Nonethless, a solid run of form including a brace of tries against Y Gorau saw him included in the Wales squad for the Autumn Internationals against the USA, Argentina and Australia. The squad were given a few days' leave before starting preparation for the USA game, which enabled Gethin to go on a whistle-stop trip to Hong Kong for the latest concert in Heledd's #HarteAttack world tour. It was there that he would meet representatives from Chinese sportswear manufacturer Nu-Wear-Now (NWN) and sign his biggest ever commercial deal.

Following the Huge Bombs debacle, Gethin had been reluctant to involve himself in more commercial tie-ups. But the fame resulting from the Lions tour and being the boyfriend of a new global pop star made some of the deals hard to refuse. With his agent Gary Johns given carte blanche to use the Huge brand where he saw fit, a tidal wave of endorsements and sponsorships ensued, including:

- Featuring in adverts for Fishch© – a vegetarian replacement for fish made of soya beans and kale, aimed at fish and chip shops
- Being the face of Woof With The Smooth©, a moisturizer for dogs
- Publicly endorsing the building of a bridge from Port Talbot to Ilfracombe

But it was the NWN deal that would cause him the most problems, leading to a chain of events that would seriously damage his Wales career. NWN, part-owned by the Chinese government, had been launched that year on the global market as a challenger to brands like Nike and Adidas and was fast recruiting leading athletes from around the world to show off their clothes.

Gethin seemed the perfect fit for the brand. NWN representatives met him in the concert interval, exchanged a few WhatsApp messages with Gary Johns, and the contract was signed before the Heledd had finished her encore.

His previous supplier was paid off and Gethin was contracted to wear NWN boots and no others for the next

25 years. A contract length of the kind only previously signed with the likes of Michael Jordan, Tiger Woods and LeBron James.

The boots were named 'The Angels' and the slogan was 'Float into Victory'.

What happened when Gethin wore them for the first time against the USA proved anything but victorious.

His Sailors and Wales colleague Tomos Maunder remembers that game well:

"I've had a couple of lows in rugby, but this has to be right down there. I've never felt more embarrassed on the pitch… What happened? Do I have to go over it again? Why don't you ask Huge? Lawyers? Okay, well, alright then…

It had been a pretty drab 15 minutes, but Owen Rhys had just gone over. Huge was on the kicks, and I could see him fiddling with his boots before stepping up to knock it over. He'd been getting stick before the game for them – they were kinda odd, in his trademark gold, but with big bulges on the side and covered in Chinese letters. I thought perhaps they didn't fit right as he was leaning down and pulling at them. Eventually he set himself and as he was stepping up to kick the ball, the ref blew up. He'd spotted those bloody wings."

The boots that Gethin was wearing had small plastic wings folded into sections on either side of them. By lifting a flap and pulling them out, they'd stick straight up about three inches. Think of when you open a page in a pop-up book. Apparently a nod to the winged sandals worn by the Greek messenger god Hermes (or "Mercury in the Roman tradition", as described in the marketing material), they were designed to make a very public announcement of NWN's entry into rugby union.

However, the designers clearly hadn't read rules 5b and c of World Rugby's kit regulations:

---

5. A player may not wear: (...)

   b. Any sharp or abrasive item.

   c. Any items containing buckles, clips, rings, hinges, zippers, screws, bolts or rigid material or projection not otherwise permitted under this law.

A pair of plastic wings protruding from either side of each of Gethin's rugby boots counted as both sharp and abrasive and a projection.

Tomos Maunder continues:

"Then the referee is talking to Huge, and pointing at his boots. I didn't notice about what. Then suddenly these stupid boots are up on the big screen. And everyone in the ground is stunned for a second, then starts laughing. The two of them are arguing, then Huge begins to jog off the pitch and the ref blows up. The kick hasn't been completed in time, so it's a scrum to the Americans. Embarrassing. Really, really embarrassing."

Gethin only has pairs of Angel boots, all with the pop-up wings. He can't re-enter the field of play so is substituted off. A howl of boos erupts around the stadium as the camera pans to him sitting zipped up in a big coat among the substitutes. Although it's not immediately obvious to the fans in the crowd why Gethin has left the field, text messages and social media soon informs them.

Wales went on to draw the game 16-16, the latest in a long line of underwhelming performances against supposedly weaker teams in the Autumn Internationals. But it was Gethin that made the headlines the following day:

FOWL PLAY! Huge subbed off in wing shoe controversy

BIRD-BRAINED
Bizarre boots cost Huge dear

ANGEL-NO-DELIGHT
Ref blast after Huge boot blunder

Chicken chow mein
Huge in hiding after Chinese boot fiasco

CHINA CRISIS "Guess I'll have to go bare-footed," Huge tells journos

A legal agreement between Gethin and NWN forbids his discussion of this incident until 2058, but he told reporters at the time:

> "I've always admired football players and their cool boots. I wanted a bit of that. I've got quick feet and thought it would be a bit of fun around that. I didn't realize the wings were illegal. I guess I'm sorry. But they are great boots. I'd recommend them to anyone looking to improve their game – they are light and responsive and made from cutting-edge textile technology as found on the Chinese space programme..."

Gethin was dropped from the squad for the remaining Autumn Internationals. Wales coach Neil Malcolm pulled no punches in his post-match press conference:

104

"I've never seen anything like it. Hughes has been good for us but this is just plain stupidity. He let himself and his team down very badly today. I've sent him back to the Sailors. I think he needs to take some time to think about his decision making, on and off the pitch."

Even friends were critical. Here's Sailors and Wales teammate Alex Anderson, playing at number eight that day:

"Huge is a mate and all, but he's often an absolute idiot. He took a ton of cash off some Chinese firm when he ought to have been keeping his head down after that penguin stuff. There were definitely some verbals in the changing room after the America game, and well, yeah – no one was that sad when Malcs chucked him out."

On returning to the Sailors, Gethin's woes were to continue. He'd signed a contract to play only in NWN Angel boots, and whilst these were illegal on the field, he couldn't play until the issue was resolved without incurring legal action from the Chinese. The WRU and the Sailors helped source some lawyers, and Gethin was sent on gardening leave whilst the issue was being decided.

"It was a bad situation, there's no getting away from it. I'd come back from the Lions with a few people thinking I was big-time, and then this happened. Honestly, I didn't realize it would be a problem. Gary told me over text he'd checked the rules and it was all good. To be honest, the money was crazy and I just went for it. I guess what happened next wasn't great either."

Whilst on leave, and while Wales were beating Argentina and blowing a 12-point lead with three minutes to go in a loss to Australia, Gethin flew out to Germany to join Heledd on the latest leg of her world tour.

Under strict instructions from both club and country to keep a low profile, he did the opposite.

Here's Edmund Givens, Heledd's biographer:

"Well, this really was at the peak of both Gethin and Heledd's fame, but in Munich it was only Heledd that was famous. That night Gethin was putting away quite a few steins of lager backstage. Heledd was always joking about getting him on stage to show the world his dancing. And whether it was his distance from the rugby world, the lager, or a combination of the two, that night he did just that."

There was no official videographer that night, so the only footage is from mobile phones. But there he is, on stage, dancing just behind Heledd during a rip-roaring version of Heledd's second hit, 'Don't Go Brecon My Heart'.

Perhaps the oddest thing about this footage is the dance itself – it is unmistakably the Macarena that Gethin is doing.

"Yeah, it's total cringe looking back. But I was pretty drunk to be honest. The whole stupid boot thing was going on back home and I was away from it all. No one wanted to talk to me about rugby. And Hels was always talking about what a good dancer I was, so I just went for it. I guess if I'd really thought about it, I wouldn't have done it. But I thought it was a laugh, and didn't think anyone would ever find out."

Within 24 hours the Welsh media was all over the story, and Gethin was once again the subject of public and professional derision.

The Sailors released a curt statement:

"The Sailors family sets the highest standards for its members, and when these standards are not met, there are consequences. Due to contractual issues regarding his match footwear, Gethin Hughes is not currently under consideration. And when his legal issues are concluded, this will remain the case for the foreseeable future."

Behind the scenes, the Sailors were less formal.

"When I got back from Munich, I was summoned to see Geert van Binder [the Sailors Manager], and yeah, he went pretty crazy at me. He had a bit of a temper anyway, but that time he was right up in my face. Out came the Afrikaans, a chair was kicked around, a pen was thrown across the room. I wasn't even offered a cup of tea. I didn't really have an excuse, so I had to take it. It was probably a mistake bringing Gary [Johns, his agent] along. And it was certainly a mistake him asking at the end of the meeting when was a good time to talk about a contract extension. The boss told me in no uncertain terms that this was not the time for that discussion. I was suspended for a month over Christmas, missing the derby games and two European cup fixtures."

The suspension for 'misconduct' would also mean that a call-up for the Wales squad for the upcoming Six Nations was unlikely.

As part of his punishment, he was tasked with doing what rugby players colloquially call 'community service' – visits to schools and hospitals, training camps, charity appearances, that kind of thing. These are pretty standard for the modern game where the professional player has plenty of free time and Gethin, like most players, largely enjoyed doing them.

The idea behind such visits was to not just give something back to the community and encourage younger fans, but also to improve the region's reputation. One school coaching session, however, whilst pleasing the attending pupils, only widened the rift between Gethin and the Sailors.

Matthew Lovering, the Sailors second row who had come through the Academy with Gethin, picks up the story:

"It was my old school, Bryn Y Felin in Swansea. I'd been back a few times as an ex-pupil, and this time I went with Huge as he'd been a naughty boy and had loads of time off. We'd take the senior XV through a training session, talk to them about a few things. It was good fun, and the boys seemed to enjoy it. The thing is, the Head of PE – Huw Pritchard – can get, well, a little physical in training. He played a bit when he was young, or so he told us, and still thought he could. I didn't actually see what happened with Huge as I was with the forwards, but I certainly heard it."

Wales World reported the incident in its own inimitable style:

WW	Sport > Rugby	F 👍 ✉

HUGE HITS!
Rugby bad boy Gethin puts hero teacher in hospital

Wayward Gethin Hughes is to be talked to by the police after a schools training session ended with a PE teacher being taken to hospital by ambulance. In the latest incident in a troubled season, Hughes reportedly hit Huw Pritchard, 47, who had a distinguished career as an officer in South Wales Police, with a tackle so hard it broke his shoulder. Pritchard, who left the force with stress before retraining as a teacher, was described as 'a big part of the school' at Bryn Y Felin, where he has taught for 14 years...

No charges were pressed, and neither the Sailors nor the school issued a comment on what was acknowledged as an accident. But this would soon change when interest in the incident reignited after a video showing the aftermath of the injury to Pritchard began being shared on social media. It might not have caught the public's attention, except that Gethin retweeted it himself.

In the video, filmed on a Bryn Y Felin pupil's phone, Huw Pritchard, clearly in discomfort, is being loaded onto a stretcher by paramedics and wheeled towards an ambulance as Gethin and Matthew Lovering look on. A crowd of boys has gathered to watch and as their teacher is being lifted into the vehicle, a chant of 'Huge, Huge, Huge' starts up. As the ambulance doors close, a loud moan from Pritchard can be heard, followed by a cheer from the boys and a further roar when Gethin turns to the crowd, giving a wink and a thumbs up.

For the second time in a month, a video of Gethin filmed on a phone and shared on social media had landed him in trouble. Asked to explain his actions to the Sailors, he repeated that it was an accident and that the smile and thumbs up was just as a thanks to the boys for coming out for the session. It certainly didn't look that way, the press once again had a field day and the Sailors and Wales high command were further unimpressed.

But now, nearly five years on, Gethin can finally reveal what happened that day:

"Well, I actually really liked those training days. I was doing a lot of them around that time as I wasn't allowed to play. We were going to the school in Swansea that Lovs [Matthew Lovering] had been to and he'd told me the rugby coach fancied himself as a bit of a tough guy. I didn't think much of it until we were going through some tackling drills. I was holding the bags and talking about technique – 'cheek to cheek', 'eye to thigh' and all that. Suddenly Pritchard, their coach, wanted a go. So I held the bag and he came full force at me, leapt off his feet and basically headbutted me. I ended up on the floor. He was standing over me shouting something about the police being the biggest gang in Wales and not to 'go messing or we'll put you down'. It was pretty mental. None of the boys seemed that surprised. Then he was like, 'Go on, have a go at me!'

So I thought, okay, if he wants a hard tackle, I can give him one. A bit stupid really but he'd wound me up. He held the tackle bag and I ran at him – I was about a step away when I saw him flinch and try and turn. I think he wanted to get out the way, but I ended up hitting his shoulder where the bag should have been. I heard the click and knew straight away he'd broken it. He was on the floor screaming and when Lovs tried to help him, he ended up pulling the shoulder further, so he just lay there swearing at me until the ambulance came. I'm not proud of this, and the video thing was stupid, but the guy brought it on himself."

When the video and Gethin's reaction came to light, he was suspended for a further month by the Sailors and forbidden from ever doing schools coaching again. Whilst his boot situation had finally been sorted – lawyers at the High Court in London having argued successfully that being forced to wear a particular shoe at work was a breach of human rights – without playing for his region, he was not selected for that year's Six Nations squad.

With no rugby on the horizon until his latest suspension was over, and not being allowed to be a part of the Sailors' community programme, Gethin had little to do apart from hit the gym and spend time with Heledd.

Her star was continuing to rise: the #HarteAttack world

tour had been extended further and the third single from *Hartebreaker* – 'Mabinogion-on-on' – was another big hit. During these heady times, it was Heledd who always seemed to navigate the world of celebrity better. Her management team sold photos of her and Gethin on holiday in Abu Dhabi, eating at a newly opened restaurant in Amsterdam and wearing his 'n' hers white denim jackets in Barcelona. Gethin was unaware of this at the time, always assuming that they were paparazzi photos rather than part of a contract signed by her management team.

Increasingly Gethin was being featured in the celebrity section of the media rather than the sports pages. A year earlier, he had been a unanimous pick in every rugby fan and journalist's Lions squad, but now between the Angel boots, the Munich Macarena and putting a teacher in hospital, he was fast approaching being a joke. Worst of all, he just wasn't playing.

A new start was needed.

Gary Johns let it be known that Gethin might be looking to start the next season at a new club, and began to put feelers out. There was interest from rugby league, with two clubs keen for Gethin to switch codes. Opportunity was also found in France and England. Criccieth RFC put in a world-record bid but, although Gary was keen, Gethin vetoed that. Ultimately it was the short trip down the M4 that won out.

Gethin would be joining the Capitol Kings in Cardiff.

He would be quitting the Sailors, the region that had given him his start, and from which he had made his Wales and Lions debuts. And whose fans had committed themselves to 'direct action' when it looked like he would be departing just 18 months earlier.

In truth, he left with not much more than a shrug. The Sailors were on course for another league title and several southern hemisphere players were already announced as joining in the summer.

> "I was sad to leave. I owed the Sailors a lot, but I just needed to get out and get my head straight. In hindsight, I should have taken a proper break or gone abroad. But the Capitols offered a great deal. I'd still be near my mum and dad, and Heledd, when she wasn't on the road, was in Cardiff. I already knew a lot of the boys through Wales, so yeah, it made sense. At the time, at least."

If the Sailors when Gethin joined had had a reputation for losing big games and disciplinary problems, the Capitols were known for big investment in players and even greater underachievement. For so long the Old Money of Welsh rugby, the resources of their owner – brewery heir Sir Edward Greenaway – were now dwarfed by Iolo Daniels' huge investments at Criccieth RFC.

In joining the Capitols, Gethin would be teaming up with Emyr Glendower Jones-Parry, now firmly established as the Wales outside half, and the top scorer in the league in what had been an otherwise disappointing season for the Cardiff outfit.

Writing in his self-help guide/autobiography, *Healing Hands and Deadly Kicks: the Emyr Glendower Jones-Parry MBE Story (Part One)*, he made clear his feelings.

> "I've known Gethin for a number of years, and he is without doubt a talented player. But I didn't think he had the right stuff for the Capitols. I remembered his antics on the Lions tour, when he disrespected Nelson Mandela. And breaking

the arm of a policeman, who I believe are true heroes without exception, is not the behaviour of a Capitols player. I did try to reason with Greens [Sir Edward Greenaway] about the signing, but I think he saw something of the 1970s era of Welsh rugby in Gethin, and that style of play. And so he joined, and of course I welcomed him, and offered him all my expertise…"

Gethin would join that summer alongside two fellow Welsh internationals, Yiannis Miller and Dylan Campbell, plus England U20 scrum half Matt Timothy and Tongan prop Siosiua Tau.

If Gethin's signing would prove to be disappointing, then nothing could prepare the Capitols for the incident that would cause such an abrupt end of Tau's career.

As the Capitols were losing the financial battle in Welsh rugby, they found themselves investing more in off-the-field activities, particularly around sponsorship and marketing. The new-season launch was always a big event as it helped boost season-ticket sales, and in 2014 it was held in the grounds of Cardiff Castle.

A whole day was devoted to the Capitols, with a sevens competition for kids in the morning, funfair, hog roast, beer tent and jousting tournament featuring 'special guests' in the afternoon, before a concert in the evening. Those 'special guests' would be five new signings, dressed up as knights and placed atop horses to introduce them to the crowd.

Matt Timothy, also joining that season from London Irish, tells us more:

"It seemed pretty bizarre from the start. But we were all new and, well, we wanted to make a good impression At least I'd been on a horse before – my sister had a pony when I was a kid.

Huge and Yiannis had done pony trekking in school. Not sure about Dylan. But Siosiua definitely hadn't. He'd only arrived a few days before from New Zealand and seemed a bit stunned.

They were trying to make it like a medieval tournament, like in the films. We all had to put a full suit of armour on and get onto a horse. The plan was, they'd announce our names, we'd flip our visors up and get a cheer, the groom leading our horse would take us for a little canter round the ground, and that'd be that.

Except it didn't happen that way – well, not for Siosiua anyway. He's a massive guy: 20 stone. They had to get special armour in for him, and I swear his horse buckled under him when he got on. Well, I went first and it was okay. Did the visor thing, then trotted around a bit. Fine. Then it was Siosiua's turn. I still don't really understand what happened, but basically his horse slipped the hold of its groom and galloped away. Slowly, as it had a Tongan prop on it. But he panicked a bit, slipped and keeled over. It was a big horse, and he landed straight on his side. Wearing a suit of armour. There was a big crash and then an even louder couple of cracks. A metal breastplate was stuck in his shoulder and his leg was twisted the wrong way around. He was screaming in Tongan – at least, I think that's what it was. It was gruesome. The paramedics had to put his visor back down and use angle grinders to get the armour off him. What a way to end a career."

Siosiua Tau's career was over. Despite his best efforts, his injuries ensured he'd never play professional rugby again. Whilst he would recover full mobility again, and receive significant compensation from both his insurance company and the Capitols, it cast a shadow over the new season before it had even begun.

On a crackly line from his restaurant in Tonga's capital Nuku'alofa, Siosiua Tau recollects the event:

"I don't want to talk about that moment as it's in the past. Though I can tell you I believe in God's plan for all. But putting a big Tongan in armour on a horse, in a field by a castle in Wales? Well, it shows He does move in mysterious ways. Sometimes very mysterious!"

Having avoided a career-ending injury on a horse, Gethin could focus on starting the new season with the Capitols. With the World Cup looming large, he was desperate to rebuild his reputation. But whilst playing time would return, controversy would never be far behind.

CHAPTER 7

International Blue

"As he pinned me to the ground, he started yelling about me talking to his girlfriend. I had no idea what he was on about!"

"Gethin Hughes is deeply sorry for any offence he may have inadvertently caused to our brave veterans of that conflict and their families…"

———————————

GETHIN'S ONE SEASON at the Capitol Kings is widely viewed as a failure.

But it started well. Very well.

After a positive pre-season, a fully fit Gethin on the eve of his Capitols debut wanted to extend his connection to rugby fans in Cardiff beyond just social media. So he took out a full-page advert in the *South Wales Echo*, paid for with his own money, stating very simply:

Cardiff,

you are welcome.

See you on the pitch

Gethin X

This unprecedented act by a Welsh rugby player was much mocked by opposition fans, including many at the Sailors, and heaped pressure on Gethin for the opening game of the season in Dublin against Leinster, who were the favourites for that season's title.

Gethin lines up in the midfield alongside fellow new signing Dylan Campbell, with Matt Timothy also making his debut at scrum half. At half time, it is 9-3 to the home team, with no indication of what is to follow. Timothy makes it 10-9 with an opportunistic tap and go, before Leinster hit back with two tries. Gethin, on kicking duty as Emyr Glendower Jones-Parry is absent with the Wales squad for the World Cup, converts two penalties to make it 23-16 with three minutes to go.

The ball is in Capitols' hands but on the halfway line when Darren Stapley slips through a weary Leinster tackle and passes out to David Naylor in space on the wing. He storms down the right flank, steps inside the defensive winger and before being clattered by the full back, feeds it inside to Gethin, who rounds the last defender and dives in under the posts to make it 23-21. The pocket of the stadium filled with Capitols fans erupts; the rest of the stadium is in stunned silence.

But within a minute, the roles are reversed.

Gethin lines up the conversion to level the scores. Kicks in front of the post are nearly always routine – sometimes they don't even get shown on television. But on this occasion, whether it is new-season rustiness, a poor connection with the ball or just bad luck, Gethin pulls his kick wide of the posts. The silence that precedes the kick is followed by a huge cheer, and then the noise of 52,345 fans blowing out their cheeks and shaking their heads as the miss is repeated on the big screen. One of Welsh rugby's most confident individuals holds both hands up to his temples and stares at the grass. He seems to be the most surprised of all.

But that isn't the end of the game.

Leinster lead 23-21 with 30 seconds on the clock. They kick off and the Capitols gather, Stapley again breaks and again slips a tackle – it looks like a repeat of the try could be on. But this time he is hit hard by Chris O'Leary and Seamus Ryan in the Leinster midfield, and pinned to the floor. For a second the referee looks like he is going to ping him for not releasing, but he manages to turn the ball. Timothy darts forward but only gains a few yards as the clock turns red. The ball comes bobbling out of the breakdown and into the hands of Gethin, who takes advantage of the broken play to ride one tackle and break into space.

Around 30 metres from the try line he has three defenders in front of him and no support runners. Gethin looks left and right as the full back's tackle is fast approaching. He has to do something.

"Well, that morning I'd been watching some of the Gaelic football on the telly in the hotel. I was watching how they connected with the ball, and remember chatting to a few of the Irish boys on the Lions tour who had played it when they were younger. Guess it came back to me later that day!"

If he's tackled, he won't have anyone to release the ball to and will be penalized.

In one fluid movement, more akin to Croke Park than the Aviva Stadium, Gethin takes one final stride, and punts the ball low, hard and direct through the middle of the posts.

23-24.

Away win.

That pocket of Capitols fans, so deflated from the miss, go crazy. The Leinster full back, whose head was just millimetres from the ball as Gethin kicked it, looks stunned. Gethin wheels away, running straight over to the bench to be mobbed by the substitutes and coaching staff.

"Huge, Huge, Huge!" can be heard echoing around the stadium, and deep into the night from some of Dublin's rugby pubs.

The Capitols have a new hero.

Gethin had not initially been considered for the Wales squad heading to Argentina for the Rugby World Cup in autumn 2014. He hadn't played rugby since the December of the previous year, and there was skepticism about whether the focus was still there after the chaos that had engulfed his last season at the Sailors.

When asked if he would be considered for the squad, Neil Malcolm replied curtly:

"We are looking to select players playing well for their regions. If you aren't playing at all, you aren't playing well."

But Gethin's heroics against Leinster and further strong performances against Y Gorau and Glasgow saw him jump straight to the top of the replacements list, and when both Eric Bolch and Rob Van Benz were forced out of the Wales squad with injury, he got the call.

Gethin was going to the World Cup.

Wales had travelled out to Argentina with a quiet

confidence in the experienced squad, for most of whom it was their second or even third tournament. In the warm-up games they'd lost to England but beaten France and Tonga, and were expected to qualify from their group, which included Australia, Scotland, Samoa and Namibia.

Gethin arrived in the camp in Palermo, just outside Buenos Aries, after they'd beaten Scotland 24-12 in their opening game. Next up were Samoa, and Gethin took his place on the bench, impressing enough in his 15-minute second-half appearance in an 18-12 victory to start against Namibia.

The southern African team were largely amateur, with only six of the squad professional. They'd lost both games heavily so far, but had underlined their reputation for physicality in putting in some huge hits on Australia and Scotland. Second row Rian Van Rooi in particular had caught some media attention for his tackling, aggressive demeanour and shock of blond hair. His day job was as a ranger on a game reserve, and in this match, he certainly had his sights on Gethin.

"We were only about three minutes in, and he came in with a tackle on me. I've never felt anything like it and I'm a pretty big target on the pitch! We had an attacking line-up, and Navs [Wales scrum half, Wayne Navden], said 'Crash this up.' I did, but I went straight into Van Rooi, who hit me harder than I've ever been hit before. I must have been winded, as I dropped the ball. A few minutes later, I was feeling okay and picked a loose ball up and headed for some space. Suddenly I felt this punch in the guts – somehow Van Rooi had blindsided me and led his tackle with his fist. As he pinned me to the ground, he started yelling about me talking to his girlfriend. I had no idea what he was on about!

But a few minutes later, as I went over for our fifth try, he landed on top of me. And out of his sock pulled a photograph of this girl. I didn't recognize her at first, then it dawned on me. She worked for South African TV and had interviewed me the day before. And yeah, she was quite pretty, but nothing happened – I only spoke to her for a few minutes. I tried to say this to him but he wasn't having it. Thank God for Zucks [Dan Nash] – I think he saved my life that day."

Dan Nash, the Wales second row that day, had grown up on a 300-acre sheep farm high in the Cambrian Mountains and is of the class of flankers who aim not to touch the ball more than three times in a match. He troubled the opposition's physio more than the scorer. He was, and continues to be, the only squad member not on Twitter, and as result has the nickname Zucks, or Zuckerberg, after the founder of Facebook – no one in the Welsh squad knew who invented Twitter. Despite his no-nonsense demeanour and style of play, he is one of the few close friends in rugby that Gethin retains.

Notoriously shy of the spotlight, he did agree to (briefly) speak to me about that game against Namibia from the family farm, where he still works in between playing and training.

"We were comfortably up on the scoreboard, but they were putting in some horrendous hits on the boys, particularly on Huge. Van Rooi was going in very hard in particular. Huge can certainly be an irritant and often deserves a tough hit, but he was getting some serious undeserved punishment that day. After one try I saw Van Rooi shouting and waving around a picture of the young lady who had interviewed us the night before. He seemed pretty out of control. So at the next breakdown, I gave him some forthright advice about his performance, and he didn't like it. So I repeated it at the next line-out, and once more a few minutes later. Eventually he snapped, as I knew he would.

He swung for me and missed, then again and missed again. On his third attempt I grabbed his arm and swung him round, pinning his arm behind him, nudged his legs and got him down onto the floor. As his teammates flew in at me, I managed to whisper in his ear and explain to him some of the farming procedures we did around mating time and how some could be practised on far bigger animals. He seemed to understand, and remained as quiet as a lamb for the rest of the game. We actually had a pint together that night, but can't remember seeing Huge for that. All good fun!"

Wales beat Namibia 82-5, with Gethin notching a hat trick of tries as well as some late conversions in a 21-point haul. Confidence was high going into their final game against Australia, the winners of which would seal top spot in the group.

Considering the negative publicity that Gethin had generated over the last twelve months, he'd kept a low profile during the tournament so far. Sporting plain black boots, a short-back-and-sides haircut and sticking to a self-imposed Twitter ban, he had for a few weeks let his rugby do the talking. Although Jon Glynn from the Borderers had the starting spot at outside centre, the consensus was that Neil Malcolm had a difficult decision approaching for the Australia game and Gethin was feeling confident about his place in the team.

"I felt really good during those first few weeks. It was nice to be back with the boys and I felt I was playing well. I also knew I had to behave myself. Killer [Ross Collier, Wales Forwards

Coach] made this very, very clear. He actually tagged me! I had this little disc with me at all times, so he could see where I was with GPS. He even told me he could give me an electric shock with it if I strayed too far. I'm pretty sure he was joking but I never tried to find out."

As with any major tournament or tour, there was media work to be done. Heledd Harte's latest single, 'The Powys of Love', had gone to number one in Argentina and she had recently played in Puerto Madryn, the home of the Welsh-speaking community in Patagonia. As a result, Gethin was much in demand by the local press. A very cautious WRU press team kept him out of the spotlight and declined most of these offers, but three days before the Australia game, they allowed Gethin to join Emyr Glendower Jones-Parry on an Argentinian rugby show on the nation's biggest sports radio channel, *Habla Deportes Radio*.

"It was just a normal interview – me and Emyr talking rugby with a couple of Argentinian guys, no problems. We were warned they had a reputation for being jokers but they were fine and we had our press officer, Natasha, with us keeping an eye on me! The interview had finished and off-air their producer asked us to record a few lines about the radio station – 'I'm Gethin Hughes, and you're listening to so-and-so station,' that kind of thing, to play as a jingle. Pretty standard – I'd done it before for stations back home. Emyr said he'd do them. He did a couple in English, then a few in Welsh for the folks down in Patagonia. But he said I should do the Spanish ones as I was more famous than him. I thought it was a bit odd, as he loves this stuff. But he handed me the lines of Spanish they'd written out phonetically and I read them out. I didn't think anything more of it and went back to camp for afternoon training.

We were going through some moves for the Australia game

and judging by the groups that we were in, it looked like I was going to be starting that game. Then suddenly, all the boys stopped. I looked to see why, and there was David Morse [the CEO of the WRU] striding right across the pitch towards me. He didn't look happy. He came up into my face, stared me right in the eyes and said very quietly, 'Get off this bloody pitch, Hughes.' I knew I was in trouble but I didn't know why."

David Morse, a QC originally from Aberporth but who had worked most of his life in London before returning to Wales for the top job at the WRU, would need all his legal and diplomatic skills in the coming days.

"I had only been in the job about six months, and the Angel boots thing was fresh in the memory for some of my colleagues. But if there's one thing I'd learnt through my legal career, it was to 'speak as you find' and when I'd met Gethin for the first time in Argentina, he was absolutely fine. Clearly a very confident young man, but I expected no problems from him. I was in a meeting with some sponsors at the hotel when Natasha, one of the press team, interrupted the meeting. She looked ashen-faced, told me there was an urgent issue and handed me a phone. I asked who it was and it was the British Ambassador to Argentina. And he wasn't happy."

"Soy Gethin Hughes y creo que las Malvinas pertenecen a Argentina." ("I'm Gethin Hughes and I believe the Falklands belong to Argentina.")

This explosive sentence was played first on heavy rotation on *Habla Deportes Radio*, then across Argentina, and within a few hours had was being heard on every news bulletin in the UK as well. The 1982 Falklands War, in which 649

Argentine and 255 British military personnel plus three islanders died, was still an issue that occasionally flared up, stoked by a few politicians in Argentina and certain right-wing newspapers in the UK. But during the run-up to the World Cup it had been barely been mentioned – most of the world had moved on. Unfortunately, this incident would bring the events of that conflict crashing into Gethin's life.

Gethin was dragged into a meeting with David Morse, WRU Head of Communications Alun Powell, and the British Ambassador to Argentina, Sir Nigel Charterhouse.

> "I honestly didn't know what I'd done. And then they told me and I just couldn't believe it. I had no idea what was on that bit of paper. I just read it out as they asked. I obviously don't think that – one of my dad's mates was out there during the war. The worst thing was, they told me that in Emyr's version of events I'd been really keen to read it out and snatched it out of his hands to do it. It was nonsense but they didn't seem to believe me. Of course I apologized but with everything else that had happened to me, I knew I was in trouble."

Within hours of the recording being made, social media had exploded with anger directed at Gethin, newspapers and bulletins were leading with the story and veterans' groups were very vocal in their disapproval, with threats to boycott the Wales national team. A picture of Gethin mocked up next to Diego Maradona, Evita and Pope Francis did the social media rounds. A Twitter poll saw him voted the second worst Welshman ever. The mood was summed up by a caller to Radio Wales, who stated that Gethin should stay in Argentina and play for them if he loved that country so much. Several more listeners phoned in to agree.

"I apologized immediately on social media, and the WRU issued a statement on my behalf. I told some journalist that I didn't know what I was reading out. This made me sound stupid but it was the truth. Then I had to do a press conference, which was awful. The journalists were asking me questions about anything but rugby. An Irish journalist asked me what I thought about Northern Ireland and I started to say something – I can't remember what now – when I felt a very hard kick under the table from David [Morse] and I stopped talking then. And just said sorry lots more. I was stood down for the Australia game and that hit me hard. I thought I'd play and I thought we'd win that one."

Wales lost to Australia 22-19, despite leading with two minutes to go. Coming second in their group meant the toughest possible draw in the quarter-final in Rosario.

New Zealand.

Gethin's Wales would face the reigning champions. The team against he had made his name against, scoring THAT try on a rainy November in 2010.

The outrage over his Falklands comments continued to rumble on, but most of the press soon realized that he had been incredibly stupid rather than callous, and eased off a little. A further apology to the British Legion ensued, with the promise of some coaching for the Welsh Guards rugby team when back in Wales. Also helpful was the diversion of media attention created by the 'Waitergate' scandal, where several of the French rugby team were arrested for drunken behaviour after their win over Italy and blamed the restaurant for spiking their drinks. A claim later disproved thanks to CCTV.

Gethin was named on the bench against the All Blacks, with the Borderers' Jon Glynn retaining his place at outside centre. At half-time Wales were 19-3 down and, as the commentator remarked, 'lucky to have three', such had been the mismatch so far. New Zealand adding a try just after the restart led to a wave of substitutions and Gethin had 30 minutes to make a positive mark on the World Cup. He entered the field to raucous chants of *"Viva* Huge" and *"Malvinas! Malvinas!"* from the Argentinians in the ground, with whom he now had a special, if unintended, bond.

Gethin immediately made an impact, intercepting an unusually lazy pass from Kiwi scrum half Darren Ke'o in the Wales 22 and running 40 metres before finding Tomos Maunder in space out wide. Maunder had an easy run in under the posts.

24-10.

A few minutes later, Gethin gained a little bit of space in the midfield and hacked on a kick into the corner. Wales pulled out one of their party pieces – a 13-man line-out followed by a 14-man drive, and Dan Nash was the player who went over the line for the try.

24-17.

Something was happening in Rosario.

Suddenly it was New Zealand who were looking a little ragged and under pressure. They collapsed a Welsh maul just inside their own half. Kickable penalty. Jones-Parry steps up.

24-20.

Six minutes were left on the clock and Wales had a scrum on the halfway line. Reset for a third time, number eight Owen Danns decided to take the moment by the scruff of the neck. He took the ball from the back of the scrum and wheeled into some open space, barging through two tackles before spinning the ball out to Jones-Parry. The Capitols outside half handed off some weak New Zealand tackling before throwing a huge pass out to Gethin in space on the wing. Catching the ball and immediately cutting back inside, a sudden glimmer of space appeared. Sprinting forward, the defensive full back Benjamin Colter hesitated for a moment as Gethin approached. Gethin threw his shoulders and sent him the wrong way but as he went past the Kiwi, Colter made a despairing lunge, reaching an arm towards Huge's legs.

In front of Gethin was open space, the posts, seven points and a semi-final.

He leapt high to avoid the contact. Colter never laid a finger on him. He landed hard on the wet turf and stepped forward. It was try time.

POP

Gethin took two more steps forward then stopped, wobbled and crumpled to the ground in agony. His knee gave way under him. A moment of surprise then relief spread across Colter's face, before he leapt onto the prone Gethin. Seconds later the referee blew the whistle. Not releasing the ball.

Penalty to New Zealand. Chance gone. Game gone. Semi-final gone.

Gethin was loaded onto the electric cart and taken off the pitch. He didn't see the remaining minutes of the game, or New Zealand scoring another try.

31-20.

Back in the medical room, Gethin and the doctors knew immediately what it was – a torn anterior cruciate ligament (ACL), which connects your thighbone to your shinbone. A very serious injury that typically requires between nine and twelve months out of the game.

"It was the worst moment of my life. With all that stuff about the Falklands, I didn't think I'd get back on the pitch at the World Cup, so to get on during that game and get that momentum going felt great. If my ACL hadn't popped I would have been away, we'd have won that game. Then it would have been South Africa in the semi-final and England in the final. Both of whom we'd beaten in the previous year. People think I'm arrogant, but I believe that had my knee not gone, Wales would have been world champions. But instead of going to the semi-final, we were going home, and I was in a lot of pain."

Gethin arrived back in Wales on 20th November and headed straight to a specialist in London to have his knee examined. The diagnosis was that in addition to going under the knife, he'd need at least nine months out of the game. The current season, after just six games for region and country, was over and he'd have to work hard over the summer and hope the surgery meant that he'd be ready for the new season.

Months of inactivity and isolation stretched out ahead. Gethin could at least spend some more time with Heledd. He had barely seen her over the previous months, the World Cup having taken him to South America, whilst a tour took Heledd to Eastern Europe, the Middle East and South East Asia.

While Gethin was being hit by off-the-field controversy and was now stalled by injury, Heledd's career was going from strength to strength. The fourth single from *Hartebreaker*, 'GLAMorgan Nites!' had been another global hit, and her provocative dance moves from the video, nicknamed by the press 'the Port Talbutt', were being mimicked in clubs around the world. She had launched her own range of vegan ready-meals, developed an app, was voted the seventh most important 'influencer' on Instagram, and would shortly be publishing both her first novel and second autobiography. Yes, Gethin was a star in Wales and in the goldfish bowl that is international rugby, but Heledd was no longer just a girl from Brecon with a YouTube channel. She was a global superstar.

Gethin, having this time gained permission from his club to make the trip after promising to stay teetotal and abstain from doing the Macarena, planned to surprise her in Kuala Lumpur, where she was playing three sold-out nights at the Bukit Jalil National Stadium (capacity 87,411).

"We hadn't really seen much of each other what with the World Cup and the tour, but we spoke on the phone when the time difference allowed, and she'd always like my Tweets. But I thought I'd surprise her out in Asia, and the Capitols were fine with it, so all good. I was just packing when I got an alert on my phone, telling me Heledd had released a new song. She hadn't mentioned anything so I was a bit surprised, but went on Spotify and gave it a listen."

The song was 'I love you so much (ft. Mitch Landers)'.

"I was excited for a second – thought wow, she's done a song for me. Then I heard the chorus…"

'No more sitting in the stands watching balls,
I'm travelling the world selling out halls.
Once I was happy with Bynea, now I'm pure California.
I don't need no rugby boy, I need a new toy.
I'm no bitch, but for me it's Mitch
Wooooo ooooooo, I love you!

The focus of Heledd's love was not Gethin, it was actor/musician/activist/poet/chef Mitch Landers, whose brand of street poetry merged with 90s grunge had been supporting Heledd on her world tour.

"So yeah, I was dumped over Spotify. Think that's a first, isn't it? I tried to call Hels to see if it was just a stunt, but couldn't get hold of her. It was her publicity manager who actually told me it was over between us. Then sent me a text with some links about the single that she wanted me to tweet, and even offered me a few quid to do so! The media went crazy about it all. I used to like all that stuff, but I was just fed up.

I just sorta slunk away, really. I didn't know what to do, so just went back to my mum and dad's in Maes-y-Tawe. I was doing my rehab, and then my knee broke down again in the spring and was told it would add another six months to my recovery. I was on Wales World, and I saw the most-read story that month was 'The 16 dumbest things Huge has ever done' – at least three of them weren't true. And I thought then, I want to quit, this isn't what I want any more."

Gethin spoke to Sir Edward Greenaway ("disappointed"), Neil Malcolm ("understanding") and his agent Gary Johns ("massively pissed off") about his decision to retire from rugby, then posted a tweet.

@GethinHughes92
That's it for rugby. Gonna take it easy and see what happens. Thanks X
Retweets 6,864 Likes 19,568

And with that, Gethin Hughes had retired from rugby. With no idea at all of what to do next.

CHAPTER EIGHT

Media (Nearly) Killed the Rugby Star

"At first I just hung out, went to the gym, ate all that yoghurt, wrote some poems, that sorta thing. But yeah, I got pretty bored early on. And then I got a call from the TV guys."

"Who doesn't know the difference between a bull and a cow? He's from Wales, for God's sake."

ASKING GETHIN WHAT it was like when he announced his retirement from the game, less than a year after playing in a quarter-final at the Rugby World Cup, fails to elicit much of a response. It's still a period that he finds difficult to talk about, but he does now acknowledge that this was a time in his life when some serious mistakes were made.

One particular moment early in those first difficult weeks away from the game would show how low he had sunk. His brother Rhys takes up the story:

"I was coming back from school one day – I'd had a parents' evening so it was about 7 p.m. As I pulled up outside my house, I saw Gethin walking up my road. He was swaying to and fro, proper zigzagging. He even bumped into a car, setting the alarm off. I thought, he's bloody drunk. I walked up to him and he looked awful, really queasy and kinda glazed over in the eyes. I'd seen him hammered before, but not like this. I gave him a bit of a shouting at as I thought he'd been drinking all day – upset over the rugby stuff and Heledd, y'know. I didn't want him like that in front of the kids so I got him into my car, where he immediately passed out, and drove to his flat. I managed to get him through the door and I was hit by this amazing smell of strawberry. We went into the living room and there were – I'm not kidding you – dozens of empty yoghurt pots, you could barely see the floor for them. I made him drink some water and he passed out on the sofa. I had to open the window as the smell of fruit and dairy was overpowering.

He'd got drunk on yoghurts. What a bloody fool."

Of all the bizarre incidents that Gethin has been involved in, being the victim of Mullerski Syndrome, an ultra-rare condition where so much yoghurt is consumed that it ferments in the stomach and turns to alcohol, creating a drunken effect, is certainly one of the most unusual:

"I can't really remember a lot of that day... As part of my contract with Yew Tree I used to get a massive box of their yoghurts delivered. I'd take it into training and the boys would all help themselves. I still got the delivery, but didn't have training. Or much else to do. I didn't want to waste them, so I started eating them. Next thing I knew, I was outside my brother's house, then woke up feeling awful the next day. I counted up the pots, and it seems I'd eaten about 40 litres of yoghurt in one day. Worst hangover ever. And I've had a few…"

These empty weeks were a struggle for Gethin. He had turned from national treasure to local joke, as evidenced by some of the comments on Twitter about his sabbatical:

@BrexitWales88 Good riddance, your shite now. H8 u!

@AJDaviesBryn Jones-Parry is much better anyway, bye bye

@BallerTownie Whats e going to do now? On the dole by Xmas I BET

@Tripper10 Gutted mate, come back soon. Still absolutely class on his day

@Welshrugbyfeet Can you send me a picture of your feet? Please. PLEASE

Twitter is no great indicator of public opinion, but after a couple of years of hijinks, injuries, a very public break-up and very little rugby, a fair chunk of the Welsh rugby public had moved on from the Gethin Hughes story.

> "Yeah, I guess it was a bit of a funny time. All I'd wanted to do for ten years was be a rugby player. Then, I guess I didn't. What I did I have on my CV apart from a World Rugby Young Player of the Year Award, a Grand Slam, a Lions Tour and seven years' worth of individual honours and awards? Some GCSEs and A Levels. So yeah, I wasn't that equipped for a break. At first I just hung out, went to the gym, ate all that yoghurt, wrote some poems, that sorta thing. But yeah, I got pretty bored early on. And then I got a call from the TV guys."

Reality TV is a regular outlet for celebrities of all calibres to earn some extra money and maintain their public profile. Gethin's agent Gary Johns, although unwilling to speak to the author, explained a bit more about how this new opportunity came up to the *South Wales Evening Post*:

> "Well, I'd always thought that Gethin would be a natural on telly – the cameras loved him when he was on the pitch, so why

wouldn't they if he was on a show? I gave the team at *Question Time* a call first – they were coming to Caerphilly soon, so I thought I could get him on that. Talk politics and stuff. They didn't call me back. I gave *Big Brother* and *Strictly* a bell, no luck with them. One show that was interested was based in Russia, where you had to be trained to be an astronaut – I promised them that Geth could learn the language in a month, but they didn't seem convinced. I was getting a bit desperate, not much money coming in for either of us. Then the farming people called and I thought, waahay, quids-in, here we go. This'll do."

The 'farming people' were the producers of Welsh agriculture-themed reality TV show *Farmer's Gold*. When they called Gary, they were recruiting celebrities for its latest series. It had been an unexpected success, launched first in Welsh, then in English, and now franchised to another 12 countries around the world. The show's premise was simple: eight 'celebrities' would move onto a farm just outside Llandeilo and, over two weeks, compete in a range of rural activities ranging from sheep shearing and tree felling through to making bara brith and organising a *twmpath* (folk dance). Points would be awarded for each one, with a live Grand Final at the end of the series to crown the winner.

"I hadn't actually watched it before. I mean, I'd heard of it, but I've never really been into that kind of thing. I'm not really a big fan of animals and that. But Gary was keen, and as I wasn't earning, neither was he – he made that very clear – and I had nothing in the diary, so I thought, sure – why not?"

Gethin was to join the series alongside an eclectic set of fellow contestants. There was ex-MP Ralph Berman; former Miss Wales Eleri Saunders; the only Welshman to play in the NHL, Gareth 'Nuts' Naughton; Welsh Children's Laureate Mary O'Hare; folk-singer and language activist Siôn ap Iorweth; newsreader Tomas Fulton and former lead singer of The Chapels, Rob Denning.

Filming began in March at Ffos Felin Farm, just outside Llandeilo. The show had made semi-celebrities out of the farmer, Aled Treharne, his wife Mair and their three teenage children, Lowri, Daf and Rhun, and their book *What's the English for Fferm?* had been a surprise bestseller the previous Christmas. Now in its third series, the producers were confident of another successful season, with hopes of franchising the show further. Little did the producers know, this would be their most challenging series yet, and one that almost ended *Farmer's Gold*.

Miriam Rivera, the show's Executive Producer, gives us some background to Gethin's involvement:

> "We were delighted to have Gethin involved. I'm not really a rugby fan myself, but he has a lot of followers on Twitter, he's a good looking lad, has no criminal record and was unemployed, so as far as I'm concerned he was perfect for reality TV. But yes, he almost got himself killed live on air, so we probably shouldn't have booked him. That said, that still wasn't the worst thing to happen on series three."

The first episode passed largely without incident. The two tasks were ploughing a field the traditional way with a horse, and then teaching an old sheepdog some new tricks. Re-watching the video, Gethin seems quite relaxed. Partnering with Eleri Saunders and Rob Denning, he shows a surprising aptitude for working with the dog, and they claim a respectable second place.

It was that night that the problems started.

All the contestants were staying in a converted stable block adjacent to the Treharne family home, and had retired back there after dinner in reasonable order. All apart from Rob Denning, an indie-music darling in the late 1990s when his band The Chapels had surfed the twin waves of Cool Cymru and Cool Britannia to considerable success and three top-ten albums. Since then, the band had broken up, as had two marriages in quick succession. When he joined the show, he was back in Treforest working on a musical inspired by Twm Siôn Cati, a Welsh Robin Hood-style figure from the 16th century.

Denning had enjoyed several more drinks than everyone else, and according to Gethin was 'going to the toilet loads and really, really chatty. You couldn't shut him up. Like some of the English lads on the Lions tour.'

Once the contestants were back in the stable block, what exactly happened next is still unclear. It seems that Denning wanted another drink, and gaining access to the Treharnes' house by an unlocked back door (it is the countryside, after all), managed to find the drinks cabinet.

One bottle of sherry later, he woke the family by bellowing out a few lines from his latest musical project.

'Ohhhhhhh, Twmmmmmmm,
You're so Welsh you're not called Tom.
If you lived now, you'd be the Bomb.
Ya better than poncey Robin Hood.
You never got caught in your wood
…Ohhhhhhh, Twmmmmmmm'

The noise wakes the family and the house erupts, Aled Treharne running downstairs shouting and loading his shotgun. Denning panics and runs out of the door and straight into the jaws of the family dog, Howley. Confronted by an angry sheepdog, a loaded gun and then the police, Denning sobers up very quickly. It's only a flesh wound, and no charges are brought. But Denning leaves the show.

> "The whole business with Rob was unfortunate. He is such a sweetie, and scored very high in our focus group pre-show, but he couldn't stay. The Treharnes made that pretty clear. A shame. The show was off to a bad start. And then the Siôn stuff began – that wasn't great either." – Miriam Rivera

Filming was adjourned for a few days, but recommenced with the second episode – driving a quad bike around an obstacle course and sheep shearing. Denning may have departed, not to be replaced, but another slice of drama would arrive in the shape of Siôn ap Iorwerth.

The 71-year-old grandfather of five has been a popular figure on the Welsh-language folk scene since the 1960s. He has 16 albums under his belt, but is still probably best known for '*Geronimo yn Ddyn Cymraeg*' ('Geronimo is a Welshman') – his 1968 song equating the Native American struggle with the battles to secure the future of the Welsh language, and made famous for a new generation when covered by the Super Furry Animals in 1997. Alongside the music, Siôn has also been arrested at several demonstrations and is not allowed within 150 m of any members of the Royal Family after throwing a buttered slice of *teisen lap* (a deliciously moist type of Welsh fruit cake) at Prince Charles whilst he was visiting Machynlleth in 2008.

> "I like Siôn – not paying attention to much outside rugby, I didn't know him before the show, but he was a good laugh

for an old fella. He swapped between Welsh and English a lot, but fair enough. A lot of the other folk and crew were Welsh speakers. So that morning at breakfast, I was chatting to Eleri – who had dated quite a few of the lads in the Welsh squad, so I knew her a bit – and Ralph the MP, who I think quite fancied Eleri… Anyway, Siôn's chatting in Welsh to Tomas and Nuts, nothing unusual, like. And the producer comes in, giving us a bit of a briefing for the day, and asks if there's any questions. And Siôn asks something in Welsh. The producer can't speak Welsh, so asks him to say it again in English. But he replies in Welsh, everyone laughs a bit, but then he just carries on. He won't speak English. And then he starts shouting and it gets a bit mad."

Unbeknownst to the show's producers, Gethin or his fellow contestants on *Farmer's Gold*, the break in filming had seen Siôn make his annual pilgrimage to the grave of Saunders Lewis: political activist, poet and one of the founders of Plaid Cymru.

You'll no doubt remember this story, but just to go over the details briefly, with a fresh zeal for the Welsh language, Siôn returned to *Farmer's Gold* refusing to speak English. He was happy to complete in the tasks, but only in Welsh. The show had originally been broadcast in Welsh, but this series was in English and Siôn's contract, which he'd signed, had confirmed that. The producers reminded him of this, politely at first, then a little more firmly.

"Siôn is such a darling. But he really was a frightful pain on this show. We tried to win him round, but he wouldn't move unless he could speak Welsh. It wasn't a Welsh-language show and most of the contestants weren't fluent so it wouldn't work, really. We were back and forth all day between Siôn and my boss down in Cardiff, but there was no budging. Then next thing we know, there's a crowd of people with signs and banners picketing the farm, and we needed to call the police. Again!" – Miriam Rivera

During the increasingly fraught negotiations, the Treharnes' 14-year-old son Rhun had been listening in, had quickly taken to Siôn and decided to publicise the argument. A few Tweets to key accounts later, and within hours #FarmersGate was trending in Wales and a crowd of nationalists and language activists were protesting outside Derwen Fawr Farm.

Gethin was once again caught in the headlights of a major scandal. The penguin, the Falklands and now this – it was becoming an annual event.

Siôn was arguing that he should be able to speak in his own language on a TV show filmed in Wales for a Welsh audience, and that subtitles would do the job. The TV producers were stating that this wasn't fair on the other competitors and would put people off watching. Plus they couldn't afford the translators.

The next 48 hours were a media storm, the furore dominating social media, making the front pages and becoming the top story on news bulletins. It quickly escalated from an argument over one show to the provision of Welsh-language programming in general. First it was just the Welsh media paying attention, then it became an international story. And Gethin was about to make a difficult situation even worse.

"It was pretty mental really. We couldn't get out of the farm – there were hundreds of people in the fields surrounding it. Aled [the farmer] was going crazy. At one point a plane flew over with a banner – I couldn't read it 'cos it was in Welsh, but it was something about American Indians apparently.

I get a bit fidgety when I'm stuck inside. So I tried to go for a run one day, and ended up in the middle of the field where most of the protestors were. They seemed alright, like, so I posed for a few photos, signed a few bits and bobs. Chatted a bit of rugby. Then carried on my way. I got in a bit of trouble for that later on…"

What Gethin didn't realize was that in one of the photos where he was posing grinning with a group of protestors, some them were holding a Welsh flag with the words *Byddin Rhyddid Cymru* written across it. This was the name in Welsh for the Free Wales Army, a paramilitary nationalist organization active in the 1960s. Loosely modelled on the IRA, it achieved some brief notoriety before its leaders were jailed or lost interest.

Within hours the photo had gone viral. The appearance of a Welsh rugby legend offering tacit support for a terrorist organization added fuel to an already incendiary situation into which Gethin had now been dragged.

Although receiving heavy criticism from some – one UKIP councillor tweeted that Gethin should return his Lions jersey if that's how he felt about the English – most pointed out he probably had no idea what it said on that flag, if he'd even noticed it.

Emyr Glendower Jones-Parry told reporters: "Gethin definitely can't speak Welsh. I used to wonder if he could even speak English."

Gethin's role in this crisis, which by now was being debated in the Welsh Assembly and had seen a question asked at Prime Minister's Question Time, only put a further spotlight on his absence from rugby.

The 2015 Six Nations was over, Wales finishing in a disappointing fourth place, with only wins over Scotland

and Italy to show for their efforts. Jones-Parry had struggled with his role of playmaker, and the post-mortems of the defeats nearly always included at least a passing mention of Gethin. Despite his issues, Gethin's absence from the game was keenly felt by Wales, on and off the pitch. And the contrast between playing international rugby and being effectively under house arrest on a Carmarthenshire farm at the heart of a Welsh political crisis was not lost on him either:

> "I did watch the Six Nations, and guess it was funny not being there. I didn't really miss all the stuff that comes around it. But the buzz of the match days, the crowds on the streets of Cardiff, having a laugh with the lads – well, most of the lads – getting all that free stuff from the sponsors… yeah, I missed it. And during the Siôn stuff, I had a lot of time to think about this sabbatical. Three years after playing for the Lions, should I have been doing a show like *Farmer's Gold*? In hindsight, no, probably not."

After a four-day stand-off, the warring parties came to a truce. Siôn agreed to speak English for most of the show if he could speak Welsh to the Treharnes, the contestants that were fluent and Howley the farm dog, who couldn't understand any English anyway. He was also given assurances of increased government funding for Welsh-language media, and a one-hour concert on Christmas Eve on S4C with funding to fly over his favourite Pueblo (a type of Native American music) act especially for it. Following the Denning sacking and #FarmersGate, the producers hoped that series three would get back to some normality.

They were wrong.

Episode four included a task focused on milking cows.

One by one, each contestant would be sent out to the field, had to round up a cow, bring it back into the milking parlour and milk it. The one who could deliver a pint of milk to the Treharnes' kitchen table in the fastest time would be deemed the winner. The important thing was to do this without help from the farmer, who would watch from the production van. The draw was made and Gethin was going to go first. A decision that almost proved fatal.

In assisting with the writing of this book, Gethin has been very candid in speaking about the incidents in his life, many of which are deeply embarrassing. But even he refuses to speak about what happened in the field that day. Aled Treharne, however, is more than happy to retell the tale:

"Well, we were doing this milking challenge, you see. What the producers want is to see the people going out on their own, and getting better – what they were telling me they call 'narrative', or something. So it was just Gethin, and Jules the cameraman. The rest of us were all watching on a little telly in the truck by the farm. So I point out the cow to milk, he seems to understand and they head off down towards the field to fetch her. We start the clock as it is all about the time. So they are jogging. Now, all the cows are in the far field, and one up from there is the field where Brutus the bull is. As Gethin gets to the bull pen, he starts to climb the gate. I guessed he was taking a shortcut. The bull was asleep but he's still very dangerous – they can get nasty, quickly. Gethin is going across the field, but not to the cows – to the bull. The cameraman hasn't gone in and is filming from over the hedge. I think he's shouting something.

By this time I'm worried. He actually goes over to the bull and starts to shake it. To wake it up! Can you believe it? By this time I'm running down to the field as quickly as I can. As

I go down the hill, I can see Gethin being chased round the field by the bull, nostrils flaring, hooves going, the lot. Lucky he was a back as I don't think a forward would have made it. He just about made it over the gate before he got caught. If the bull had got him he would have stuck him and that might have been that. Gethin was shaking afterwards, in a bad way. I asked him what on earth he was doing waking a bull. He said he thought it was just a big cow. But that he'd always wondered why it was on its own in the field. Who doesn't know the difference between a bull and a cow? He's from Wales, for God's sake!"

Even now, watching the clip of Gethin's brush with death at the horns of Brutus is shocking. First him stroking the bull to try and wake it, then nudging it, then full on pushing it. Even Gethin's biggest fan would agree it's a remarkably silly thing to have done. There's a precise moment when the angry and confused bull wakes and glares at Gethin. It is clear on the video that this is the moment that Huge realizes he's in real trouble and begins to back away. The joke was that he hadn't run that quickly since his debut try for Wales against New Zealand, evading the bull by just inches as he hurdles the gate.

The video of him, eyes wide and terrified, running towards safety, was leaked almost immediately on social media and quickly became a sensation, gaining over 15 million views at the last count and adding a further facet to the legend that is Gethin Hughes – but a second or two slower, and that could have been the end of the story.

With the video released, the story became big news. Gethin was again the subject of ridicule from across the media, with the tabloids going to town:

UDDER CHAOS Wales star's brush with death on Farmer's Gold the latest disaster for TV show

'A TOTAL AND UDDER IDIOT'
Farmer's blast at Wales legend

UnbelievaBULL! Rugby star Huge cheats death after mistaking bull for cow

Cow-nt yourself lucky!
Huge just inches from death on Carmarthenshire farm

WHAT A MI-STEAK!
Brutus the bull almost has a Huge dinner

Gethin's run-in with Brutus the bull was the end of his time on *Farmer's Gold*. He was, according to his family, very shaken after this experience and to this day has an aversion to farms and avoids all beef and dairy. Despite the pleas of the producers, who were delighted with extra publicity this incident had created, Gethin quit the show. Like Rob Denning, he too would be an early leaver from series three.

"It was a shame to see Gethin leave – he was a real sweetie. But the bull thing could have been very bad for the show. And him of course. But with the Siôn stuff and the clip of him running across that field, what we'd done was already going to make the show a smash. We'd like to have him back, though – if we ever do an All-Star version, I'll be straight back on the phone."
– Miriam Rivera

By quitting *Farmer's Gold*, Gethin had forfeited a large chunk of his fee. And money was getting short. He was still living in a luxurious Cardiff Bay flat, and although he'd earned decent money during his Wales days with appearance fees and bonuses, a mixture of rash investments, some expensive holidays with Heledd and R S Thomas first editions had left him needing the money from his remaining sponsorship deals more than ever. Most had not been renewed in the months since he'd retired: sports brands aren't interested in paying you if you don't wear sports clothes any more.

And Gary Johns was finding it difficult to gain much corporate interest in a retired rugby player who had fallen out with management and teammates and was now most famous for almost being skewered by a bull in Carmarthenshire after mistaking it for a cow.

So, with his finances increasingly parlous, Gethin's sponsorship with Welsh yoghurt maker Yew Tree Dairy (name since changed to Dragon Vale Dairy) was crucial. Unfortunately, his work with them would lead to yet another near-death experience and media storm.

As part of his agreement, Gethin had committed to engage in the promotion of Yew Tree's 'Good moo-rning' campaign, aimed at getting more people to have yoghurt and other dairy products for breakfast. As part of this, a number of Welsh celebrities would eat breakfast at various famous landmarks around the country.

So, *X-Factor* winner Will John would eat his in Caerphilly Castle, BAFTA-winning actor Mel Stringer on the Mumbles Pier, Siôn ap Iorwerth at the Owain Glyndŵr memorial in Machynlleth, Emyr Glendower Jones-Parry insisted on the Principality Stadium ('my second home'), and Gethin was ordered to the top of Snowdon, Wales' highest mountain, 1,085 metres above sea level.

June 9th was designated 'National Welsh Breakfast Day' and all the celebrities had to be in their positions and eating dairy-based food by 8 a.m. to ensure maximum media coverage. Gethin was ordered to do some tweeting and then a phone interview with a local radio station when he'd arrived at the peak. He was joined by one of the Yew Tree PR team and set off at 5 a.m. carrying a small fold-up table, chair, tablecloth, yoghurt and a six-foot balsawood spoon strapped to his back.

What happened next has again gone down in Gethin Hughes folklore, so over to the man himself to tell us in his own words what happened:

> "Well, we were having to get to the top of the hill for the yoghurt stuff. Get up there, few pics, couple of tweets, quick call from a radio station and back down again. Nice and straightforward. But the fella I was with, Joe from the PR company, was telling me he knew a shortcut from when he'd been up there doing Duke of Edinburgh with school. He seemed to know what he was talking about so I thought fair enough, I'll follow him. Anyway, next thing I know we seem to be walking away from the top, and then some rain and mist starts coming in."

Gethin and Joe Parker, from Cardiff Bay-based Perci PR, had both failed to check the weather forecast for that day and although it had been bright when they had set out, they hadn't realized how quickly weather could change on the mountain.

> "We keep on walking but the weather begins to get really bad, I keep checking my watch, and it's coming up to eight in the morning and I'm worried we aren't going to make it. Joe begins

to panic, saying he's still on probation and starts to sorta run. He goes about 100 metres, then goes over on his ankle. I hear a crack. He's bloody broken it! So we're lost on the side of Snowdon, he can't move so we're stuck, and it's getting really misty and rainy. And I've got this six-foot spoon strapped to my back. We can't see a thing. I'm not sure what to do – and next thing I know my phone goes. It's the bloody radio station…. I try to style it out, pretend all's cool but they can hear Joe moaning in the background. I have to tell them straight that we're in trouble. They keep us on the line for ages, talking away, and well, you know the rest…"

The call came in from the breakfast show on Radio Caernarfon presented by Daz Michaels and Llŷr North. When I spoke to them for this book, they looked back on this episode as being a real highlight, this show still being the most listened to in the station's history. Here's an extract:

Llŷr: Welcome back to Radio Caernarfon! And we've been teasing you all morning that we have a very special guest…

Daz: Yes, that's right – all the way from Snowdon we have Wales and Lions legend Gethin 'Huge' Hughes live on the line.

Llŷr: Good mooooooo-rning, Huge (*Farmyard noises playing in the background*)

Daz: Cow you doing, Huge? (*Canned laughter*)

Gethin: Ha, ha… very good, boys. Hi, yeah, I'm good thanks. On top of Mount Snowdon.

Daz: What you doing there, then?

Gethin: Well, as we all know breakfast is the most important meal of the day and… (*muffled cry in the background*)…

Llŷr: What was that noise?

Gethin: Nothing, just the wind, anyway so the best way to start the day is with a *(a louder cry)*

Daz: Who was that? Who's up there with you?

Gethin: Oh, just Joe, he's helping me with this. *("…arrghh, this really hurts!")*

Llŷr: He sounds in pain – are you OK?

Gethin: Yes, I'm fine. As is Joe. You see we've both had a great breakfast of Yew Tree Dairy yoghurts and as a res… *("…get help, I need help…")*

Daz: Huge, what exactly is going on?

Gethin: Errr…

Finding they had an exclusive on their hands with a Welsh icon stranded on the side of a mountain live on air, Daz and Llŷr were initially reluctant to involve anyone else in their scoop. They kept talking to Huge for another 10 minutes, even getting him to read out a weather forecast and pick a song. But eventually one of the station's listeners became concerned and called Mountain Rescue. The weather had deteriorated further, and an urgent message went through to the RAF rescue team based at Valley in Anglesey.

Prince William was at the time still stationed at RAF Valley, and the future Prince of Wales would now be called upon to rescue a man once considered Welsh rugby royalty.

At this point the visibility was so poor that Gethin and Joe didn't see the bright yellow Wessex helicopter piloted by Flight Officer Wales until it was right above them:

"It was pretty mad, really – we were shivering and cold, and Joe's leg was in a bad way. I was starving, but even then I didn't want to eat any of the yoghurt we had after my overdose earlier in the year. I poured some on Joe's broken ankle hoping it would freeze and become like plaster. But that didn't help. Our phones were dead and we were soaking through. Then suddenly this massive yellow helicopter appears, and Prince William is flying it! I thought I might have been hallucinating. But no, not this time. I'd actually met him on the Lions Tour, but didn't expect to see him again like this! They winch up Joe, then send a line down for me. The RAF guy tells me to chuck the spoon away but the dairy told me it cost £120 and that I'd better not lose it. He tells me to stop being stupid. But money is tight, y'know. So I put it on my back and get winched up."

That dramatic moment of rescue was caught by a fellow climber, and the famous photograph of Gethin being winched into the helicopter by the heir to the throne with a massive spoon strapped to his back was on most of the front pages the following day.

And for the second time in a few short months, generated more embarrassing headlines for Gethin:

MOUNT SNOWDUMB
Disaster-prone rugby ace rescued from PR stunt

HIS ROYAL HUGENESS
PRINCE RESCUES FORMER WALES
LEGEND FROM MOUNT SNOWDON

Silly hillbillies
HUGE AND PR PAL BLASTED FOR LACK
OF PREP FOR MOUNTAIN CLIMB

Taken back to the RAF base, Joe was sent to hospital, and Gethin was checked for exposure before being asked for a selfie by Prince William. The photo, on which Wills used the hashtag #TwoPrinces, generated over 100,000 likes – and disapproval from some senior members of the Royal Family.

His retirement, the bull incident and now this latest embarrassment had made Gethin the butt of a national joke. His glory days with the Sailors, Wales and the Lions seemed a world away.

As a result of the fiasco on Mount Snowdon and his failure to complete his task, he lost his contract with Yew Tree. Now with no discernable income aside from a small royalty from his book of poetry, he was in effect bankrupt. No longer able to afford his rent, he moved into his brother's spare room. It was a new low.

"Yeah, it was pretty shit. The thing on the mountain was bad, but not my fault. Although a bit of me was relieved to have escaped all the yoghurts. I've not eaten one since. But it left me with very little money. My brother's great, and offered to put me up. He hadn't actually checked with his wife, but I think that was cool in the end. So yeah, there I was, unemployed, skint and with my career over. I had no idea what would happen next. I had to get a real job."

CHAPTER 9

Huge No More

"Listen, you brain-dead idiot, you do what I say or I'll end you.
You stupid-shoe-wearing, farm-safety-ignorant waste of space."

"Why did I invite him in? Do you not remember him?
He was a fantastic player. Yes, he had his ups and downs.
But he never let me down. It was good to see him. The lads
loved it too. He's still a hero to a generation. Don't forget that."

WRITTEN IN HUGE lettering on the wall of Bae FitnessX in Cardiff Bay are the words of Drax Drooman, the ex-US Marine who brought the global exercise phenomenon to Wales: 'You can feel sore tomorrow, or you can feel sorry tomorrow. YOU CHOOSE!' For the uninitiated, FitnessX is a training programme that builds strength and conditioning through extremely varied and challenging workouts. It was founded in 2000 in California but one of the areas in the world with the most franchises is South Wales. And it was Bae FitnessX, run by ex-Capitols number eight Charlie Ferrer, that Gethin joined in 2016 as an instructor – his first ever 'proper job'.

"I didn't really know what to do when I retired. I was thinking of
going to university, but wanted to get my head straight before I

did that. I knew Charlie a little bit and I did some sessions there. We got chatting, and I ended up doing an instructing course and went from there. I actually quite enjoyed it, and it paid enough for me to move out of my brother's and rent a little one-bed flat in Splott. I was kept pretty busy – Charlie made a pretty big deal about me working there and it drummed up quite a bit of business, and lots of people always wanted to chat about rugby. Then about six months in, I took on Roger Sherlock as a client and well, it all went a bit nuts."

Roger Sherlock, Welsh Assembly Member for Abertillery, was 57 at the time he began working with Gethin. One of the most familiar faces in Welsh politics, his family legacy stretched back to volunteering for the International Brigades in the Spanish Civil War via the Miners Strike, contributions he was always keen to highlight when on the election trail.

He'd first met Gethin in his role as Minister for Culture, Tourism and Sport, though he was Cabinet Secretary for Local Government and Public Services when he signed up for Bae FitnessX, which, being just ten minutes from the Welsh Assembly building in Cardiff Bay, listed several AMs and many more staff among its members. Followers of Sherlock's Twitter account were treated to regular photos of him working out with Gethin and selfies of the two of them regularly adorned his Instagram (with hashtags including #WelshLegends, #FitnessXers and #DynamicDuo). This blossoming bromance between politician and retired rugby player would soon come to a shuddering halt.

"He was a bit of a funny one. He'd always be massively intense in the sessions, but then always moving his sessions around, cancelling at the last minute and just turning up randomly at other times. It was hard to keep track of him. But I just thought it was him being busy and all. Then one day someone called from the Assembly called and said he worked with Roger, and wanted to check some of the dates of his recent sessions. I was in the middle of doing the big shop in Tesco and asked him to call me back later. A few minutes later, Roger called and he sounded super stressed."

The call was later used in evidence, and can now be revealed for the first time in public.

Gethin:	Hiya Rog, wassssssup!
Roger Sherlock:	Listen Gethin, has someone called for me?
Gethin:	Yeah, just –
Roger:	What did you say?
Gethin:	They just want to check some dates of your sessions – I told 'em to call me back.
Roger:	Right, good, good. Okay, if I tell you some dates, can you tell them I was with you?
Gethin:	Errr…. I guess… why?
Roger:	It doesn't matter. Just do it, please.
Gethin:	Well…
Roger:	Just do it.
Gethin:	Who are they?
Roger:	It doesn't matter.
Gethin:	Well….
Roger:	Listen, you do this or I'll make you pay.
Gethin:	What are you on about?
Roger:	Just f***ing do it, Gethin!
	Listen, you brain-dead idiot, you do what I say or I'll end you. You stupid-shoe-wearing,

farm-safety-ignorant waste of space. If you want to carry on being a FitnessX trainer, you listen to me…

Gethin: To be honest Rog, I'm not that bothered about the FitnessX stuff. See ya around.

CLICK

It turned out that Roger Sherlock had been engaged in selling government-owned farmland at significantly below market value to a group of Malaysian businessmen, and had received a substantial backhander in the process. His sessions with Gethin and regular cancelling and rescheduling was to help create alibis for his nefarious activities. It wasn't only Gethin who had been used like this, either.

Sherlock's Zumba class had covered for one extra marital affair and a badminton club for another. A professed preoccupation with pottery had helped give him time to submit hundreds of fabricated PPI claims, whilst stamp collecting supposedly took him to fairs around the country, when actually he was selling timeshares in Spain. The Welsh public, while appalled at his actions, by the end of the trial had a grudging respect for the number of hours Sherlock had been putting into things that weren't his job or his family.

After a year under the radar, the 2017 trial of Roger Sherlock brought Gethin back into the spotlight as a witness for the prosecution. Whilst Gethin struggled to accurately recall the dates of their sessions, Sherlock's love of meticulously documenting being #FitAndFabulous as part of #TeamHuge on social media eventually blew his alibis apart and he was sentenced to three years in jail. As he was hauled out of the dock, he hurled abuse at Gethin, with whom he seemed most angry:

"You stupid f**k, I could have had a my pick of ex-Welsh players as FitnessX instructors but I choose you. You were meant to just go along with it all…"

Bull-S**T Sherlock – crooked AM gets three years was the pick of the headlines the following day.

Whilst Gethin was appearing at Cardiff Crown Court, his former teammates down the road at the Principality Stadium were struggling. A comfortable home win over Italy had raised hopes of a good Six Nations tournament, but that would be their only win. The week that Gethin was testifying against Roger Sherlock was when the Wales squad was preparing for a crunch fixture against England. In another world he would have been in Surrey prepping for the biggest fixture of the year, but in this world he wasn't. Wales lost 19-9.

"It was a weird time – I'd sorted of ducked out of the spotlight. I wasn't going to any rugby things, not doing any interviews, I even eased off Instagram and Twitter. Now that I was trying to be an ordinary working man, I even joined LinkedIn! The court case was going on when the Irish boys were over. I'd been sent to get some soya lattes for Charlie and the other instructors when suddenly I bumped into the lads I knew from the Lions tour down around the Bay. We had a good chat, a few jokes about old Pat Mandeville, and as they were heading off, Rory Fitzgerald said he was glad they weren't playing against me the next day. That kinda hit home a bit. In the goldfish bowl here, all I'd heard was Welsh opinions, but him saying that made me think about what other people thought about me."

Wales would lose 28-12 that Saturday, narrowly avoiding the Wooden Spoon in 5th place.

Roger Sherlock was in jail.

Heledd Harte was on a 36-month global tour with her fiancé Mitch Landers.

And Gethin was just another FitnessX instructor picking up shifts when he could.

One man who hadn't abandoned Gethin was his agent Gary Johns.

"Yeah, Gary still stuck with me. I'm not sure how it happened but he was taking 15% of my FitnessX earnings too. He said he'd got me the job, though I can't remember that. He sorted out a few other bits – I did some removals work, a bit of landscape gardening, cleaned a few gutters, stuff like that. And I'd always have to give him a share. I remember I helped a neighbour out, cleaning some windows, and she gave me £20 as thanks. Somehow he found out and texted me, asking for £3."

When not getting Gethin to do odd jobs around Cardiff and the Vale, Gary was still fielding offers. Rugby clubs were still interested: French and English teams made offers to get Gethin back into the game in Union, whilst League once again got in contact to try and lure him to the north of England. Producers of reality TV shows continued to call. Gethin was offered opportunities to join fellow celebrities learning how to synchronized swim, brew craft beers, operate a crab shack in the Florida Keys and even manage a poodle parlour. He refused them all.

He even declined the chance to play a completely new sport. Gethin was invited to be a captain in the Cnapan Superleague, which Iolo Daniels tried to launch in 2017. A revival of the early type of football found in medieval Wales, it was seen by the billionaire as both a solid business opportunity and one that would give Wales a unique sport. But recruiting teams that needed over 50 members, a lack of agreement over the rules, kit and even the pitch – plus most of Wales' inability to pronounce the name – quickly made Iolo lose interest. His next project, a zoo full of animals once native to Wales but now extinct in the country, such as bears, wolves and coal miners, opens in Criccieth in 2023.

Throughout 2017, Gethin will admit to having had no interest in watching, reading or talking about rugby. But some very personal criticisms stung him out of his torpor and slowly began to rekindle his love of rugby.

In Welsh media circles, Jac Prendergast is known as The Whale, as he swallows up any job in his path. One of the most famous faces in Welsh media, he began his career doing traffic and travel updates on the early breakfast show on BBC Radio Wales and in the decade since then has increased his output to a total of six different radio and TV shows a week, plus writing a column for Wales World and regularly posting 30 tweets a day. Such is his commitment to work that he took a course in meteorology so he could read the weather in addition to the news, sport, traffic and travel on his morning radio show. He'd even tried to enter Celebrity Welsh Learner of the Year, before it was gently pointed out to him that he could already speak the language fluently.

Through his various media projects, Prendergast considered himself close to many of the Welsh rugby squad. He'd got to know Gethin quite well at his peak, and had several times asked to write his biography but always been turned down. Rugby books had become quite a lucrative side project for Prendergast: he'd ghostwritten Emyr Glendower Jones-Parry's biography, another for retired captain Will George (*George and the Dragons*), and had just written one about his own experiences in Welsh rugby.

Called *The Sixteenth Man: My view from inside Welsh Rugby*, it promised to be a 'tell-all exposé' of the last decade in the sport. The title came from how an unnamed player had supposedly once described Prendergast, and the book's publication was met with groans from the Welsh media but keen interest from rugby fans.

Although now retired, Gethin loomed large in the book, with his various travails – the Loch Ness Monster incident, the Angel boots, the Lions penguin, the Falklands controversy, among others – all featuring heavily. These stories were the ones that were serialized on Wales World and used to promote the book. One particular aspect of Gethin's time in the Wales camp was detailed at length by Prendergast.

> "Gethin's pre-match ritual was a thing of legend. Now let's remember, there are plenty of Welsh players who view conditioner with suspicion. But he lived by the motto 'look good, play good' – and would take this to extremes. Yes, the rumours are true: he shaved his legs. Yes, he used fake tan. He had a 12-step skincare routine in the morning. He was once spotted, pre-match, walking around the changing rooms with a face pack on. And received a rollicking from Killer during the World Cup for filing his nails with an emery board during a team talk."

Gethin didn't disagree with any of this:

> "Well, it sounds a bit silly, perhaps. But 'look good, play good'? Yeah, that's right, as far as I'm concerned. If you aren't happy with yourself, how are you going to enjoy being on the pitch?

And if you look good and play good, they pay good, right? Plus, it wasn't 12 steps. It was 13. There's one thing I used to keep quiet – snail mucin! What's that? Oh, you must try it! I import it from South Korea. It's basically the slime from snails, which helps cells produce collagen and elastin, which evens out skin tone and smooths its surface…"

Prendergast's book also revealed that one player used to smuggle Kettle Chips up to his room on tour after the Wales team dietician banned them, and that another 50+ cap veteran got so nervous before games he'd need the toilet six times in the ten minutes before kick-off. It also gleefully assessed several players' long-dormant MySpace accounts, and the bad language and even worse music taste and adolescent poetry contained on them.

No one would ever call Jac Prendergast the 'sixteenth man' again.

If they ever really had.

Someone like Gethin, who was never able to keep his indiscretions secret, wasn't particularly embarrassed by these revelations, but he was upset by the idea that he was never committed to the team.

The book quoted one unnamed Wales teammate:

"When Gethin was focused and on form, I must admit he was good. But he was only ever really committed to one thing, and that was Gethin Hughes. Whereas I am the ultimate team player, always considerate of my actions, and something of a philanthropist off the pitch, he certainly is none of those things. Yes, I am highly educated. Very highly educated, in fact. He is not. I am from Cardiff, a global city. He is from somewhere in the Swansea Valley, I think. To be honest, I don't even know where that is. I'll never go there. So, yes – he had the talent, but he didn't have much else. And some of the scrapes he found himself in? Well, I'll never forgive him for his disrespect to Madiba…"

This criticism goes on for three pages as the individual, a teammate of Gethin first with Wales U20, then Wales, the Lions and most recently the Capitols, really opens up to Prendergast about what are some clearly deep-seated feelings about his former colleague.

Whilst Gethin quietly stewed on this criticism, his mum did not stay silent. Her post on Facebook quickly went viral.

"I've read what he's said about @Geth and I think it's disgusting. Yes, he's made mistakes, but haven't we all? I've met the person who wrote this – he hasn't hidden himself very well. And I'll tell him exactly what I think of him when I see him next. And let me tell you: he says Gethin's underachieved? A Grand Slam, 24 Wales caps, a Lions Tour, a Celtic League Winner's Medal and a World Cup Quarter Final: if you think that's underachievement, well, you don't know much about rugby. @MikeHughes and I are so proud of you, Geth. XXX"

The summer of 2018 saw Gethin take to the rugby pitch for the first time since that World Cup Quarter Final nearly four years earlier.

Along with the FitnessX training and the usual mix of casual labour for Gary, in the spring of 2018 he'd started doing some work for the Sailors, visiting the Academy and talking to some of the younger players about the importance of making correct decisions off as well as on the pitch.

The region had quietly announced they were working with Gethin, drawing some criticism from their fans, who thought he was the last person who should be offered the chance to work with their players.

But Geert van Binder, still prospering as Sailors Manager, was steadfast in his support:

"Why did I invite him in? Well, I am South African, and we know something about truth and reconciliation and how important it is. Do you not remember him? He was a fantastic player. Yes, he had his ups and downs. But he never let me down. It was good to see him. The lads loved it too. He's still a hero to a generation. His mistakes were off the pitch. Don't forget that."

Gethin puts it a bit more bluntly:

"I was like those druggies who used to come into school. But it wasn't 'Don't do drugs, kids'. It was 'Don't sign deals with Chinese sportswear companies or date pop stars'."

His return to playing rugby was unintentional. Each summer, the Sailors would host a sevens tournament at the Gnoll in Neath, open to clubs across the region as well as for a select few further afield. All for charity, it attracted a good crowd, and with food stalls, a bustling beer tent and live music, it proved a lively and fun event.

One of its famous traditions was a kicking competition. An open field of contenders would take kicks from an increasingly difficult array of angles and distances until a winner was found.

Kickers from the 24 teams were to start, but in summer 2018 it was a little different. The host of the competition, local DJ Jazzy James, wanted to broaden the field and having spotted Gethin in the crowd, invited him to join the competition. Initially he declined, but James was doing the urging with a microphone from the centre circle. An image of Gethin shaking his head and trying to sink down into his seat appeared on the big screen.

As he shook his head, a round of boos echoed around the ground. James reminded Gethin that it was for charity. There was a pause, then a wry smile from Gethin as he stood up, followed by a big cheer. As he reluctantly trotted down the stairs, another familiar face appeared on the big screen: Emyr Glendower Jones-Parry, who had been there to watch the Capitols team. He hadn't been invited, but he too was now running down to the pitch.

Gethin was wearing just trainers, shorts and a Maes-y-Tawe polo shirt as he was actually there to support his brother, who was playing for them. He remained coy on rumours that he'd already had a few pints that afternoon. Emyr, however, was in full kit and boots – which, considering he wasn't there as a player that day, surprised some of the other contenders.

26 competitors – 4 academy players from the professional regions and 20 amateurs including PE teachers, policemen, joiners and IT consultants from the Sailors area, the current Wales outside half and a FitnessX instructor – begin the contest.

The first kicks are taken from the 22 line, and then move back five metres each time. After four rounds only seven players remain.

After the 6th round, the kicks are taken from 52 metres and it's just Gethin and Emyr remaining.

Gethin goes first, slipping a little in his trainers, but it sneaks over.

Emyr follows: success.

57 metres.

Gethin is successful, as is Emyr.

62 metres out.

Gethin scores. As does Emyr.

Every man, woman and child in Gnoll is utterly engrossed. The bars and food stalls are all empty as everyone is focused on this battle. Young boys have climbed trees to get a better view. Someone has launched a drone from the car park. People are streaming the competition though their phones. Twitter is going berserk. S4C have even interrupted their coverage of the *Solo Recitation from the Scriptures for those aged 16 and over* at the Eisteddfod to show this duel.

This is big.

In 1986, Paul Thorburn converted a penalty kick from 64.2 metres out during a Five Nations game against Scotland at Cardiff Arms Park. That remains the world record.

The next kick in this competition is 67 metres out.

Gethin steps up.

He takes a deep breath, runs his fingers through his carefully waxed and set hair, takes a dozen steps back, turns to the camera and winks, before hurtling himself head down towards the tee and giving the ball an almighty whack. It's very hard, it's very low and it's very good. Over it goes.

The crowd goes wild.

Emyr looks unperturbed. He goes through his well-practised routine, addressing the ball. He makes a fine contact and it too looks good. And then it's not, falling short by a few metres.

The crowd goes even wilder.

"Huge, Huge, Huge" echoes around the ground. It's almost like old times.

Gethin looks a little more tired than he used to in his playing days, but gives the crowd a big smile and lifts up his arms in approval.

Emyr storms off down the tunnel. As he does, a TV microphone picks up what sounds like a middle-aged woman with a very soft Swansea Valleys accent shouting, 'Why don't you stick that in a book, Emyr?'

That night, the drinks went on late into the night. Gethin was back in the rugby environment for the first time since the World Cup, the Gnoll clubhouse being full of the Maes-y-Tawe squad and former teammates, as well as coaching staff, from both the national team and the Sailors. Songs, laughs and stories echoed deep into the Neath night. Gethin even did the Macarena, complete with all the moves. Now that was really like old times.

"It was a good night, alright. First time I'd enjoyed being in a rugby crowd for a long time. It was probably about four in the morning and I was walking across the car park towards my taxi when I heard someone moving in the shadows. I turned and peered into the darkness then I heard the voice: 'Good Evening, Mr Hughes' – it was Killer. He'd been waiting for me all night. I thought, oh, here we go. I'm in for it again – I was pretty drunk, after all. But he said well done, and that I'd played well. He said I should come back to playing and that he could help with it if I wanted. I was stunned. I wish I could remember exactly what he said. But I do remember his last words to me that evening: "You're still an idiot though, Hughes – now go to sleep."

The following day, Gethin was awoken by a flurry of messages from an excited Gary Johns – his kicking duel had gone viral, and the offers were flooding in. It wasn't just the skills on show that excited the clubs, it was the response from the fans in the ground and around the world. Gethin was still box office. This time Gethin was keen to come back. He was listening to offers.

@GethinHughes92
Okay, think it's time I got the boots back on X
Retweets 918 Likes 2,709

Iolo Daniels came in with a huge offer, written on a scroll and delivered to Gethin's brother's house by Iolo's personal peregrine falcon. Super Rugby wanted him. Leinster came in with a dazzling offer and a promise to build a dynasty around him.

@GethinHughes92
Decision made. Will tell you tomorrow X
Retweets 11,239 Likes 3,676

Welsh rugby was at fever pitch. Wales World ran a story confirming he'd rejoined the Sailors, then retracted it and stated he'd signed terms with Y Gorau. *The Guardian* said he'd be joining Saracens, as *The Times* reported he was already training with Stade Français.

All would be wrong. As always, Gethin didn't do what everyone thought he would.

@GethinHughes92

Delighted to confirm I am rejoining @MaesytaweRFC. Training still Tuesdays and Thursdays at 7pm right?

Retweets 14,532 Likes 5,690

Ten years after making his first-team debut for the club, former Wales and British and Irish Lions star Gethin 'Huge' Hughes was back playing for Maes-y-Tawe, in WRU Division 5 South Central (C) of the Welsh pyramid.

And he couldn't have been happier.

Author acknowledgements

EVEN A SILLY little book like this one wouldn't have been possible without the support, help and love of a lot of people.

Most of all I'd like to thank my mum and dad. It was my mum that first took me to St Helens to watch Swansea RFC – standing on the terrace cheering Simon Davies, Scott Gibbs, Kevin Morgan and the rest is among my favourite memories of a very happy childhood. My dad is not just a keen rugby fan but has also has an artist's eye for Wales' culture and its people. I hope that this book shows both a genuine love of rugby, and an affectionate if sometimes mischievous look at Welsh life.

A huge thank you also to my wife Eimear for the encouragement to actively pursue my idea after talking about it for so long! And once I'd started, for helping me carve out the time to actually do it – during the writing process we didn't just move house but also had our first baby. So this is for little Iseult too, who was an extra motivator to make this book as good as it could be... although her preference is currently to chew rather than read books!

Massive thanks also to the fantastic, hard-working and supportive team at Y Lolfa. In particular to Lefi Gruffudd for reading my speculative email, picking up the phone and giving me this opportunity. And to Carolyn Hodges for her unwavering enthusiasm and making me believe I could actually write this. I definitely couldn't have done this without you either! *Diolch i'r ddau*!

I also want to say a big thanks to all my family in Swansea and London – Jamie, Lucy, Pablo, Marion, Elliot, Oscar and Daphne for all the laughs, love and late-night chats! And to all the Monahans in Ireland for the same!

A big shout-out also to the 23rd Old Gorians – as fine a panel of experts on Welsh life, culture and rugby as you'll find anywhere. 6 p.m. at the Pilot, yeah?

And a final big thanks to all the real-life rugby players for making me so happy on so many occasions. Long may it continue.

Thanks for reading.

Luke Upton
September 2018
@MrLukeUpton
LukeUpton84@gmail.com

All mistakes in the text are mine and mine alone. The story, all names, characters and incidents portrayed in this work are fictitious. No identification with actual persons, places, teams or products is intended or should be inferred.

Also from Y Lolfa:

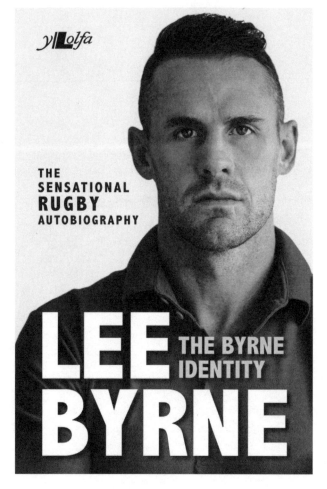

£9.99